DOG DAYS

NOTES OF NECROSOPH

AL K. LINE

Copyright © 2021 Al K. Line

Early Morning Blues

"Dad! DAD! There's a man in the hall. A burglar! Get out! Shoo! Help! Dad!"

I shot out of my tatty recliner and knocked over a delicious glass of Pinot—don't judge, I had good reason to be drinking at 7AM—as I raced towards the hallway from the living room.

Awoken by the screams, Woofer leaped up from the murder rug. I tried to step over him, but he moved at the same time, so I trod on his tail. My needy Lab yelped, I stumbled, and as he ran off, bewildered, I skidded on the rug, tripped over the bunched-up corner, and careened headfirst at the stove. I cracked my temple on the corner of the cast iron beast, gripped it for purchase, then hauled myself up and dashed out into the hall. I was dazed, and utterly bewildered, but more than ready to kill anyone who dared intrude on my family's sanctuary.

Knife already in hand, I grabbed Jen where she stood, terrified, in the open doorway and pushed her behind me then readied to destroy this lowlife.

"Oh, it's you," I said, relieved. Adrenaline dissipated and I was left with nothing but a throbbing head and a sense of disorientation.

"Why is it so bright?" The *man* squinted and put a meaty hand up to shield his eyes.

"Because it's daytime. In the summer."

"Is it always like this?"

"Um, yeah. Usually."

"Glad I've never bothered then."

"Yeah, me too." I fastened my knife back in its sheath and sighed as I felt my head. A massive lump was already forming.

Woofer wandered over and sniffed perfunctorily, then trotted off, uninterested. They'd met a few times; Woofer was nonchalant about him for some reason. Probably because they were a similar size and he never got any attention, not even a hello.

"What's going on?" shouted Jen. "Who is this... er, man? Is it a man? What's happening?"

I scowled at the idiot in my hallway and turned to Jen, my beautiful princess dressed in her school uniform. "Hey, it's okay, no need to worry. Everything's fine."

"He's in our house. He scared me. Who is he? Why is he here?" Jen sniffed and wiped away the tears.

"Sorry, sweetie, please don't get upset. Don't cry, there's nothing to fear."

"But who is he?"

"Annoying." I turned back to him and scowled. He shrugged his shoulders, then at least had the sense to find his glasses and put them on.

"This is Shey Redgold of Oxten. He's, um, how do I put this?"

"I'm a dwarf an' I live in your basement. Me an' your dad have bin friends for over sixty years after I saved him from certain death. I saved his life, that's what I did."

"Now, that's not exactly true," I told him. "You know that. You were running away after nicking loads of gold, and happened to swing your axe and cut my bonds. That's not exactly heroic."

"No, but I still saved you," he said, scowling from underneath enough hair to open a wig shop.

"And I helped you survive, and keep all that lovely gold, didn't I?"

"What are you talking about?" yelled Jen. "What is this? Dwarves, gold, saving each other from other dwarves. And he isn't even sixty!" Jen wagged a finger at the myopic dwarf. "He's loads younger than that!"

"No he bleedin' well ain't. That'd make him a child. A teeny-tiny child. Us dwarves aren't even adult then, still babes. Like you. What are you, forty or summit?"

"No, I'm eleven. Argh, what is happening?" Jen put her hands to her temples and shook her head. I think she was somewhat surprised. It was understandable - dwarves don't appear in your hallway very often. At least this one didn't.

"Sorry, Jen, this must be a bit of a shock to you. I don't want you to feel threatened. Shey Redgold is a very old friend." I shot him daggers. "And, um, that other stuff? Guess we better have a chat about that. But first, let's make the introductions properly. You okay?"

"I'm... yes, I suppose. Dad, this is nuts."

"Honey, you have a dragon. You have a unicorn. Our cat is immortal. He named himself Mr. Wonderful. You talk to the dog. Grandma is a witch. You fly when riding Bernard, and we have a troll on the lawn. What's so weird about a dwarf in the basement?" I grinned at her as she smiled, then chewed at her lip.

"Guess I've never thought about it much. Just the way things are." She shrugged, like all good young Necros would.

"Exactly. But I'm sorry, I should have told you about Shey Redgold."

"Of Oxten."

"Oh, shut up!" I told him. "Yes, alright, of Oxten. Like anyone knows where that is."

He pointed down and smiled smugly.

"In our basement?" asked Jen.

"No, deep down in the bowels of the earth where the dwarves live. My home, where I was happy for many years before a slight misunderstanding. Now I live here. It's nice. I have my gold, and it's dark."

"You have gold?" Jen was suddenly all ears.

"What? No! Who said gold?" Shey Redgold fidgeted and panicked, looking shifty as hell. He was ready to run. I'd seen it before. "I didn't say gold. Did you say gold? Cause I never. No gold. None. An' if there was, it'd be mine. Hands off. Not that there is any. So, this is the human world, is it?" he said, changing the subject, and looking at the floor, walls, lamps, and whatnot. "What do you do?"

"How'd you mean? " asked Jen, her fear gone, now just utterly fascinated to be having a conversation with a four-foot-nothing dwarf draped in leather and chainmail.

"You know, what do you do? Up here? Fight? Count your money? That's what you have, ain't it? Money? It sure is bright. Makes my eyes hurt."

Jen moved closer to Shey Redgold and studied him properly. He stood there, nonplussed, checking out our uninspiring hallway.

"Um, let's go into the living room and have a chat," I told them. I gave the dwarf another glare as he bumbled past, following Jen.

"What's all this then?" he asked.

"It's our living room," I told him. "We chill out, relax, play games, watch TV, that kind of thing."

"What's TV?"

"It's this large screen here," said Jen, amused, as she pointed at it.

He stared at it for several minutes while Jen and I snickered, then he sighed and said, "I prefer watchin' my gold. Um, if I had any. Which I don't."

"Not when it's off, silly," said Jen. "When it's on." Jen picked up the remote and turned on crappy morning TV. A load of women sat around talking about some other woman in a movie or something. Boring!

Shey Redgold's eyes lit up. He plonked himself down in my chair—yes, *my* chair!—laughed when it reclined, then just stared at the TV, seemingly utterly fascinated.

"I think you better turn that off," I told Jen. "Don't want an addict."

Jen nodded, and pressed the standby button. The dwarf moaned, then rubbed at his eyes after removing his glasses. He replaced them then heaved out of the recliner and beamed. "That was awesome! What's it called again?"

"TV." Jen crouched and looked at him. "So. You really are a dwarf?"

"Well, I'm short, I have a very impressive beard, I own an axe, I like to dig, an' I do love gold. But I don't have any!" he added hurriedly.

"Honey, he is a dwarf. He lives in the basement and always has. That's why I have a key and you have never been allowed down there."

"I never really thought about it. It was always locked and when I was little you said it was dangerous, that the stairs were broken."

"A white lie. And we will have to talk about my age, and some other stuff, later, but for now, I have one question. Cover your ears, Jen, just for a moment. Please?"

Jen raised her eyebrows but did as I asked. I turned to Shey Redgold and roared, "What the fuck are you doing out of the basement? You utter dwarfy dickhead."

"Just wondered what the human world was like. Fancied a peek. I, er, picked the lock an' came out. Then this girl, your daughter, was there, screaming, so I didn't know what to do. I like it. Bit bright, but I like the TV. Can we put it back on?"

"No way. You can't just pop up like that. It's our home."

"Mine too. I live here too."

I fought down my frustration. He was right. "Sorry. Yes, it is your home too. But please ask before you just turn up. It's polite."

"You don't ask before you come into the basement to get your foul wine. You turn on the light, blind me, then swear at me. An' try to steal my gold."

"I do not steal your gold."

"Only because I catch you."

"That's a lie! I—"

"Can I move my hands now?" shouted Jen.

I turned and nodded at her. "Sorry, our visitor was just saying he won't do it again. And he has to go now."

"I don't. I want to watch TV. What do you eat up here? Got any mead? Let's have the tour then."

And so, on one of the most surreal mornings of my life, my eleven-year-old daughter and I gave a truly ancient dwarf who had lived in my basement for many-a-year a tour of our home.

He wasn't impressed.

He hated the carpets—said they weren't natural even though they were wool. He disliked the bathroom—he had a real aversion to water. And he thought beds were for idiots, as who would choose to sleep on something that soft when gold was perfect for sleeping on and so much better in every way.

Phage called up the stairs for Jen to get a move on. It was time for school. We both checked our watches.

"Time to go, my little apple. Don't want to be late."

"Not so little any more," she said, smiling, still utterly bemused by the whole situation.

"No, I suppose not. How come you've gone from being seven and tiny to eleven and almost as tall as me in what seems like a day?"

Jen stood on tiptoe and kissed my cheek. "Happy birthday, Dad. Love you. Nice meeting you, Shey Redgold," she said, her smile faltering a little.

The dwarf nodded gravely. "You too."

Jen shot down the stairs and we followed. No point trying to hide this from Phage.

"Hello, Phage."

"Oh, erm, hello. You're, ah, out."

"Yes, but it wasn't worth it. Apart from the TV. I think I like that."

"Oh, yes, well, okay. Bye, Jen."

Jen waved at us then was out the door. She was old enough to cycle to school on her own now. Another hard-to-accept part of having children and them refusing to stop getting older.

"Bye, love. Have a good day," I called after her. She waved without turning and then stopped. She rushed back in, snatched her school bag, grinned sheepishly, then closed the door behind her.

There was an awkward silence, then we both turned to confront our morning visitor. He was gone. I shrugged and went to get another wine. It was only once a year, and you know I had the right.

Miserable Men

"What on earth is he building over there?" asked Phage, as we peered over the high hedge into my neighbor Job's property—you pronounce it Jobe if you value your tongue.

"No idea. He's being super-secretive about it and a right smug bastard too. Four bloody years he's been at it. I figured he'd have caved by now and spilled the beans." I'd asked him every time I saw him, which, thankfully, wasn't that often, as he made me seem like a happy-go-lucky kinda fella. Job took being a miserable old bastard to the next level. Guess he'd had over four hundred years to perfect his technique.

We peeked through overgrown hawthorn, careful of the rotting posts holding the stock proof fencing, trying to get a proper look at the small copse of trees in the meadow and the towering structure Job had been constructing at random times of the day and night for what now felt like an eternity.

"I can't see properly," said Phage, craning her neck forward like that would somehow make a difference.

"Let's just go visit him. Say hello. Maybe if you're with me he'll take pity on us."

"Do I have to?" whined Phage. "He's such a grumpy old sod, and he seems so angry to see me. Like I've done something wrong."

"Haha, don't take it personally. He's annoyed to see everyone. Come on, it'll be fun. He said we could pick as many flowers as we wanted. He even hates them. Calls them 'bastard weeds' right to their pretty little faces."

"Well, maybe... Oh, okay, let's do it!" Phage grinned at me like a naughty schoolgirl, as though we were doing something bad and bunking off school.

"That's the spirit," I told her. I felt happy, light, free. Grounded in a way I couldn't ever recall. For the better part of a year I had done nothing but relax and enjoy life. There were several weeks of utter stress after Phage had her note, as when she returned she was in a rough way both physically and mentally, but she recovered quickly, and the year had basically been a great one.

Four years had passed since I'd had my double-whammy of notes, and in the intervening years the work had been gross, yes, but nothing like the previous notes. I killed on auto-pilot, tried not to dwell on my despicable actions, knowing I trod a dangerous path by not accepting the foul deeds I'd committed, but if it meant I retained my sanity, then I'd go with it and sleep better for it.

Yes, for once, I was a rather chipper bloke who just so happened to commit the odd murder when I was so directed. We also got a swimming pool, which helped. Fuck, this heat was unbearable.

Giggling like our daughter, Jen, as she'd opened her birthday presents three days ago, we hopped over the fence, battled the unruly wilting hedge, then stepped into paradise. At least, you could call it that if you ignored the piles of baths, the rusting tractors and farm machinery, and the endless stacks of pallets and general crap that signified the land of a man definitely no longer interested in maintaining a working farm. His loss, our gain. For one, it was quieter, apart from the weird construction project, but mainly because the many acres Job owned had outshone themselves this year.

The wild flowers were an assault to the senses in every way. The drier the UK got, the more parched the land, the longer the days, the crappier the air, the better the meadow did. Blood-red poppies stood tall and proud, spires of rattleweed shone as bright as the sun. Daisies and endless varieties of native wildflowers created a kaleidoscope of carpeted magnificence almost too intense to look at for long.

And the smell, oh the smell. It was intoxicating, dizzying, and beyond delightful.

"I feel drunk," giggled Phage, as she skipped through the meadow, spinning in circles with her arms spread wide, turning fast to take it all in.

"See," I laughed, "told you it was worth braving the wrath of Job to come visit him more often. We'll pick some of these beauties on the way back. Let's go see what he's up to in the damn copse."

"We can't do that," Phage whispered, suddenly serious.

"Why not?"

"We're trespassing. We have to go tell him we're here. Ask him if we can take a look."

"He won't mind."

"He bloody well will. And you know it. And what if he doesn't know it's us and begins blasting with his shotgun? Have you seen him with the crows? He's mental."

"Okay, fair point. Let's go say hi. We need to thank him for Jen's present anyway, although she'll have to come herself and say thanks too."

"I'll bring her around later, to his front door, just so he doesn't accidentally shoot her or throw a hammer in her face."

"Good idea."

Hand in hand, we wandered through the meadow, past the junk covered in creeping bindweed, and up to the large, decrepit barn where Job spent most of his time when he wasn't building mysterious structures in his tiny forest.

We heard him before we saw him.

With the air blue from such creative use of British swear words, we approached the barn cautiously, ready to duck if any tools came flying at us.

"Job," I shouted. "Job? You in there?"

"Of course he is. We can hear him," Phage told me.

"Um, yeah, I know that. It's just what you say. You know, to be polite."

"I don't think you need to bother." Phage nodded at the angry old man stomping out of the barn with a club hammer in one hand, a beer in the other, and a mighty fine scowl on his lined face. He glared from under bushy yellow eyebrows then downed his beer, threw the bottle in a pile, and took off his hat and wiped at his sweaty forehead where lank hair was plastered.

"What the fuck do you pair of bastards want?"

"Blimey, been practicing for the swear Olympics, have you?" I chortled.

"Fuck off, Soph. I'm busy."

"Aren't we all?"

"No, you aren't. Neither is she. Hi, Phage. You look pretty."

"Oh, thanks. That's nice of you to say."

Job shifted uncomfortably from foot to foot, fiddled with his hat, stared at the hammer like he hadn't known he was holding it, and looked genuinely surprised he'd given a compliment. I think it was his first.

"Yeah, well, I'm trying to relax, be nicer."

"Good start," I told him, smiling.

"Fuck off."

"Not so good," I mumbled.

"Look, I'm busy. If there was nothing else?" Job turned to get back to his business.

"We haven't said anything yet," I protested.

"You've said more than enough. I know, you wanted to say thanks for Jen's present, ask if you can pick the flowers, and were thinking about sneaking down to the woods to see what I'm building. Well, yes, take all the bastard flowers you want, but no, don't go near the woods. There are traps, so nobody peeks. You'll get yourselves very killed, very fast."

"Job, what if Jen goes there by accident? Or Woofer?" protested Phage.

"Tell them not to," he said, with a shrug.

"You are such a kidder," laughed Phage nervously. You just never knew with Job.

"Oh, I'm fucking hilarious. Now, anything else? Would you like a cup of tea? Slice of cake? Boot up the arse?"

"Yeah, what are you building?" Phage blurted. "It's been four years now. Surely it's finished?"

"Nope, got loads more to do. All will be revealed when it's done. Now, bugger off." Job swung his hammer about as though to punish the air as he muttered to himself and stomped into his barn. He slammed the huge door shut behind him and instantly upped the swearing as he whacked things and made them pay for the crimes he insisted they'd committed.

"Let's go pick the flowers," I told Phage.

"He's such a funny guy," said Phage, eyes sparkling with amusement.

"Oh, hilarious."

We held hands as we walked back through the meadow. Phage picked a massive bunch of flowers and I stared at the looming mess of wood and steel that poked above the trees like a treehouse from hell itself.

What was the old bugger up to?

The Truth About Cats

"You ready for the onslaught?" asked Phage, eyes gleaming with malicious delight.

"No. Why can't we do a birthday party like the other years? Stuff outside?"

"Because she's eleven. And eleven-year-olds don't want bouncy castles and jelly and ice-cream."

"No, I know. And I was told as much by my darling daughter. Although, I think it might be an imposter. A doppelgänger. One who refuses to turn off lights, and swears you told her it's okay to wear skirts that are actually bandanas in disguise. How did she change so quickly? One minute it's all, 'Ride horsie', the next it's being moody and arguing about make-up. I mean, did you see the clothes she wore the other day? In my time she'd have been, well, I don't know what would have happened, but... Ugh, I just wished she'd stay little."

"You get it easy. I'm the one who takes her clothes shopping, has to decide what make-up she can have, what music she can download. It's a bloody nightmare. Not to mention all the other stuff."

"I know, and you're awesome at it. Best mum in the world." I put my arm around Phage as we walked through the paddock at the far end of our piece of paradise and towards the barns, outbuildings, stable blocks, and assorted enclosures that made up the zoo and the property as a whole. Luckily, I'd done my chores for the day, so could hide out while Jen had her friends over for the night. A sleepover, her first, and I was not looking forward to it.

Not only because I couldn't even begin to imagine the nightmare that was about to ensue when five young girls got together in my house, but because today was my birthday and it meant only one thing.

Necronote.

It was late, and I didn't like late. I liked to get terrified, battered, maybe sliced up a little by the yearly note, when I first awoke. Not have to hang around all day waiting for it to arrive.

The only good thing about this year was I could get going early in the morning and not have to rush. Having to fit in a murder around the day of the week your daughter's birthday happens to fall on had been tough, but now she was older and the parties had stopped, it meant I could pretty much begin my torturous hunt straight away.

Although, obviously, I'd rather stay and listen to a bunch of kids bang on about how unfair life in general was, theirs in particular.

And yet, I still felt chipper. What was with that? Normally, the day was full of dread. My guts cramped, I needed the toilet repeatedly, and wasn't the best of company. Maybe it was because Jen was so happy despite the constant moaning and bickering. More than that, it was because the development of her gifts had slowed right down while her body went through other changes.

She hadn't begun whispering, using magic to mess with the world, hadn't suddenly taken on Phage's abilities, which both of us absolutely dreaded, and she was yet to get into loads of trouble with her absolute best friends of the non-human variety, Tyr and Kayin.

She was just my little girl, with gifts developing like many others in her situation, and it made us all happy. Jen undoubtedly knew more than she had, understood there were things going on she wasn't privy to, that she would change as she grew older, but my daughter was a sensible girl despite her years.

The apple of my eye told nobody she had inherited her father's zoolingual abilities, that she owned a unicorn she'd named personally, and one day a young wyrmling would accompany her on trips to murder a stranger, as she absolutely did not know that was a thing. I prayed she never would. Of course, I knew once she was a little older we needed to sit her down and somehow explain that every year once she turned twenty-one she would be expected to head out into the world and most likely kill a person she had never met just because it said so on a note. And if she refused, she would die.

Until that time, Mum and Dad, no longer Mummy and Daddy, just went on mysterious yearly trips that she ached to have explained but never did.

"Go and put your feet up. She won't be home for a while. I've got stuff to do in the kitchen. Don't forget, make —"

"I know, make myself scarce once they arrive. Let them use the living room to watch movies, and don't get annoyed by the noise. You got it." I pecked Phage on the cheek, then wandered into the scene of future crimes committed by wailing children, and eyed my tatty brown recliner greedily. Maybe a little doze before the onslaught began? It better bloody come before the kids arrived. Didn't want daemons prancing around while they gossiped about boys. Their parents would have a fit.

I settled back into the recliner and rubbed at my beard. I'd thought it would be nice to grow one again, but it was peppered with as much silver as my shoulder-length locks and made me look older than I was meant to, so I would probably shave it all off.

Feet up, practically horizontal, I sighed and let myself relax.

Thwack!

The catflap slammed shut, followed by a terrible wailing. A moment later, it banged again. All hell broke loose. Mr. Wonderful hammered into the living room, pounced onto the window sill, launched at my head, clawed my face, jumped into my lap, and dumped something wet and shining on me. Then he almost flew onto the cabinet under the TV, threw himself into the air, did a three-sixty, and with claws extended, evil look of death-personified on his furry white face, proceeded to sink his claws deep into the side of a black cat I'd never seen before in my life.

Shocked, and utterly bewildered, I scrambled to my feet, the thing on my lap fell to the floor, and the black cat dashed out of the room and presumably through the catflap. Mr. Wonderful sprang after it, only to return, nonchalant, in seconds. He ambled along, smiling, then sat on the rug in front of me and said, "I found a piece of paper."

I glared at the folded piece of paper on the rug beside him, then back at him. "What is it? Where'd you find it?"

"How should I know what it is? It's for you."

"How'd you know it's for me?" I asked, feigning ignorance, my guts already tight, my teeth grinding. The mother of all headaches pounded behind my eyes.

"It's got your name on—"

"Stop," I sighed. "I can't do this again. Let's cut the crap. I am not playing this game any longer. I know what it is, you know what it is, so let's forget this charade. And who the fuck was that? You nearly killed the poor guy."

"He was on my patch. He's encroaching. This is mine." Mr. Wonderful waved a blood-stained paw at the world in general.

"Okay, whatever. You can bugger off now." I eyed the note nervously.

"What the hell's going on in here?" shouted Phage, as she stormed into the room, looking worryingly like her mother, not the forty-seven-year-old that only looked thirty-five that she was.

"Sorry, Phage," said Mr. Wonderful. "I was..." *slurp, slurp,* "...just seeing off an intruder."

"Stop licking your fucking balls!" I shouted at him. "Sorry, love, he said he was seeing off a cat intruder. And he brought me my note," I said, glum as only a man in my situation could be.

"Oh, sorry. Have you read it?"

I stared at the squirming note then snatched it up with a creak of my knees. "No, just about to. You go back into the kitchen. Don't want you hearing me swear, and maybe blurting something I shouldn't."

"You sure?"

"Yes."

"Okay. And Soph, I know I've said it before, but I really am sorry about the other year, when I forgot. She's doing well now, isn't she? Our little girl."

"I told you, it's fine. And yes, you're doing a great job. Nobody could do it better." I nodded and she left.

Mr. Wonderful stared at me with his usual look of utter pity because I wasn't him, then sauntered off to see what else he could terrorize out in *his* world.

"Thanks for the support, you bastard," I said, once he was out of the room. This is the problem with cats that you can communicate with—you can't say anything bad to them because they understand you and will then proceed to shit on your bed. Or in your slippers. Or piss in your drink when you aren't looking. I'm not joking, it happens to every person in the world who lives with a cat.

I flopped back into the chair, put on my glasses, and stared at the scrawled calligraphy.

Necrosoph.

How I hated reading that name. How I hated the black ink splodges, the rushed nature of the writing. Knowing I had no choice, I unfolded the slightly damp, thick paper and read the contents.

"Weasel. Kite." It was the fucking app thing again. I grabbed my phone, took it out of the improved dragon-proof, water-proof, and daughter-proof case, then tapped in my password and fired up the Necroapp. "Stupid bloody idea. I want proper coordinates, an address," I muttered to myself, just because it was what I always did.

The stupid wheel thing spun around and around, thinking, then the app sprang to life and zoomed in on a location. A simple flag marker gave me the exact spot I had to reach to fulfill my duties. Then the image zoomed out, put another marker at my location, and gave me the distance.

"Fucking Liverpool? That's miles away." Looked like more Necros had died, as this was not my usual patch. Every year it got larger. Every year the job got harder. Every year more of us died.

I had several choices, depending on the road I took, ranging from fifty miles or so up to almost seventy. As usual, I'd take the quieter roads if possible, just to keep stress down, not hit as many checkpoints, and because I'd have a dragon with me. Plus, I liked the country, and there were more places to get shade. But Liverpool? Ugh, this was not good.

I turned off the app, locked my phone, then put it back in the case. Didn't want nosy girls *accidentally* seeing things they most definitely ought not to see just yet.

The note squirmed in my hand, just to screw with me, so I grabbed it, ran out into the kitchen past a startled Phage, and into the back garden just in case anything kicked off. I held it at arm's length, waiting, but it settled in my palm and stilled.

"Okay, yeah, that's more like it," I said to the paper. "Cool, no daemons or wraiths, or buggering about for a change." It was always nice when nothing freaky happened. I waited another minute, then pocketed the note securely, and just stood there, slowly calming down and rubbing at my temples.

"Oh my god, oh my god," came the shrill, mortified voice of my daughter.

I ran back inside as fast as any father hearing his daughter in distress would, and straight into the living room. I crashed into the back of Phage and was greeted by five young girls all pinching their noses and staring aghast at the murder rug.

"Don't ever call me a bastard again," said Mr. Wonderful smugly, as he sauntered off, leaving a massive cat turd behind as a *gift* to us all.

Jen had the sense not to get into an argument with the cat in front of her friends, because that would be utterly weird, and besides, he was gone.

"Anyone fancy a beer?" I asked with a sigh.

"Dad!"

"What?"

"We're eleven. Oh, hi. Did you have a good day?" Jen stood on tiptoes although she didn't have far to reach and gave me a peck on the cheek.

"Thanks, honey. Yeah, great. So, that beer?" I asked, smiling.

"I'll take one, Mr. Blaine," said a pretty girl with raven hair, black eye-liner, and a studded choker around her neck.

"Haha, sorry. Maybe in another century or so. Well, see you. Have fun." ·

"Dad, what about that?" Jen pointed to the pile of poo on the rug. I stared at it, sure there was a tiny mouse face peering out of it.

"I'll sort it. Girls, give me five minutes to fumigate the place," said Phage, "then you can hang out in here. Have the place to yourselves. Watch movies. You can order pizza later. Okay?"

"Yes!" The girls punched the air and giggled, then began jabbering about what to watch and how many pillows they would need, and could they sleep in the living room too, and stay up late watching horror movies.

I winked at Jen when she caught my eye; she smiled back at me.

I buggered off to the pub.

Woofer Want to Come

I exited via the kitchen back door to the shrieks and screams of young girls pretending they were all grown-up. It was hard to adjust to such sudden shifts in behavior. A few years ago she wore sparkly unicorn swimsuits and wouldn't eat her dinner unless Tubby Teddy sat in a chair too, and had a proper setting including food and water. Now she wanted Doctor Martens and her belly button pierced. I blamed the internet, and the government, and books, and other stuff I knew I should know about but didn't.

But she was a good girl, and was now incredibly strong and proficient in all manner of useful things. Archery, climbing, screaming about not getting her own way, picking unsuitable clothes, gymnastics, swimming, holding her breath under water, communicating with other animals, ignoring her mother, and most importantly of all, still giving her dad a kiss goodnight. Would that ever stop? I hoped not.

"Help! Woofer want to come to pub too," shouted man's best friend, as the now seven-year-old Labrador hurtled out of the door with his tail tucked between his legs and his ears flat against his head.

"Haha, don't you want to hang out with Jen and all her friends? I thought you loved that kind of thing? All the attention."

"Want to dress Woofer in tutu and put colors on fur. Woofer hates perfume too, and Twilight is on TV. There's three! Three!" Woofer howled in pain at the thought.

"Welcome to the world of young girls," I told him. I rubbed behind his ears and he perked up. "Come on, let's go to the pub."

We strolled down the lawn, now little more than dirt and dying grass, past the chicken compound, through a gate, took a right, and there we were. Necropub. I made the sign myself. Although the door and oak cladding had seen better days, it fit with the general vibe of decay and dying brain cells, so I'd stick it out as long as I could. I opened the door and let the stale air hit me, improving my mood as always. We wandered in and I turned on the lights so it was just gloomy and depressing, rather than pitch black.

"Soph?" asked Woofer.

"Yes, buddy?"

"Is Woofer old now? Will Woofer die soon?" He stared up at me with eyes so sad I almost burst into tears. His fur had hints of silver, his teeth were yellowing a bit, and his hips ached now and then if he got wet. "Well, you aren't as young as you once were, but you're only about seven now. So, plenty of years left. Nothing to worry about."

"But Soph is so much older. Can Woofer live as long? Be with Soph and Phage and Jen forever? Like Mr. Wonderful?"

"I'm sorry, but it doesn't work like that. I wish it did, I wish with all my heart it did. But it doesn't."

"So Woofer will die soon? Just a few years?"

"Yes, you will. But you shouldn't think about that, you should focus on all the great times we've had. All the sausages you stole, the lovely walks, the adventures, all that good stuff. But listen," I bent down to his level, "you are maybe halfway through your life, so that's like being a middle-aged person, so you have more adventures ahead of you that you will remember, than you have already had. That's not so bad, is it?"

"Woofer loves sausages." His tail wagged, but his heart wasn't in it.

"I know you do. Good boy."

"Soph?"

"Yes, buddy?"

"Can Woofer come with you now? You said many years ago that I could come with you when you got a note. Help. Be there for Soph. Can I come this time? Otherwise, I will be too old, or I will be dead." He hung his head so low his tongue was on the ground and his ears were flat against his skull. His tail drooped and he wagged it morosely.

"We'll see. Like I have always told you, I don't want you getting hurt. It's dangerous out there for a dog. I don't want to risk my best buddy in the whole wide world getting killed."

"But Woofer will die anyway." He slunk off to his bed underneath the dartboard, about as pitiful a sight as I had ever seen.

Bloody hell, what's got into him? I wondered. He wasn't known for his existential crises. He wasn't known for thinking much of anything. Woofer was a dog I'd found by the side of the road when he was approximately two. I got him fixed up, took him home, and he stayed. Simply by being around the rest of us, and some of the gifted animals, he'd become able to not only communicate with me and other dogs, but with other Necros too. It didn't make him smart though, just meant he had more animals to talk to.

But he'd been out of sorts lately, moping about, and maybe it was because I had never taken him with me. Or maybe he truly did fear death.

I wondered if there was anything I could do. Anything I should do.

"Woofer?"

"Yes," came the sad reply.

"You have never told me about what your life was like before you came here. Before I found you by the road with your leg broken. Do you remember that I did that? That I took you to the vet and they fixed you right up and you came home to live with us? That Jen insisted you sleep in her room for months and months? Do you remember all that?"

Woofer wandered back over, limping, going for the pity act so he'd get his own way. He didn't know who he was dealing with. I was about as tough and cold-hearted as they came.

"Woofer remember some. Remember the vet and being saved, and sleeping with Jen. And some of what came before."

"Hey, what is it, buddy? What's wrong?"

"Make Woofer sad." His head was low again and he whined.

"It's okay. I'm here now. There's nothing to worry about. You know we all love you, right?"

Woofer nodded. "And Woofer love you. Before was bad. Lived with cruel man. Beat Woofer. Called him bad boy, smacked his nose, kicked him. Locked Woofer out for days. Woofer hungry, didn't know about roads. Got hit by cart and lay in gutter. Thought Woofer would die. Not called Woofer then though, called bad names instead."

"Makes me sick," I sighed. "Why would someone have a dog then treat it like that? Bastards." I hugged Woofer around his neck and shed a single tear for my poor buddy.

"Woofer can come with Soph?" he pleaded.

"Okay, you can come. But you must promise to be careful. Nothing dangerous. And you promise to do as you're told?"

"Woofer promise."

My lame dog then proceeded to run laps around the room, whooping with delight, head held high, tail even higher, panting and smiling and drooling and not looking at all like a dog who might be embarking on the last major outing of his life.

"How's the leg?" I asked, laughing.

"Woofer feeling much better," he said, then collapsed, exhausted, on his bed. Sometimes I think he was playing me.

"So much for the tough guy act," I muttered, then turned my attention to the three beer taps gleaming behind the bar.

"Hmm, what shall it be today?" I mused.

"Maybe I can be of assistance," came a voice I really didn't want to hear.

"It's him!" shouted Woofer. He ran for the door, whacked into it because it was clearly closed, careened back, jumped forward, pressed down on the handle, raced out, then slammed it behind him.

I turned from his antics and confronted the one and only. The Brewer.

Happy Birthday

I leaned back against the door and breathed deeply of the fresh, dry air outside the Necropub. The beer had been nice and cold, a very unusual taste, but so far I wasn't tripping my nuts off, hemorrhaging blood, or panicking about liquid excrement running down my legs, so it was all good.

I shuddered at my ordeal. A whole hour with the Brewer!

Happy to be alone, and alive, and still even relatively sane, I wandered around our main garden, looking at the flowers, admiring their ability to survive in the strange heat, then went to see what Phage was up to and try to avoid the youngsters   last thing they wanted was me around.

Phage was in the kitchen sorting out drinks, Woofer was being a dick under the table, the lightweight, and a heady aroma of pizza tickled my nostrils. I sniffed, and followed the scent.

The living room was a disaster zone based heavily on pillows, cushions, and too much cheap perfume, but the boxes of pizza were open and being devoured so I nabbed a few slices, much to the protestations of young ladies, then beat a hasty retreat with Phage out into the garden again with a nice glass of wine in hand to chase the beer.

We munched on pizza and drank expertly while staring at the "statue" Jen used to climb all over.

"I like him," said Phage, through a mouthful of thick crust. Cheese hung down past her chin. She licked it up. Nice.

"Me too. Mrs. O'Donnell hates him. You hear that? She hates you," I told our silent sentinel. I winked at him, and slowly, ever so slowly, the head of the troll turned.

"Gosh, he's frisky. I've never seen him move so fast," said Phage.

"Sometimes he gets like that. Once, I saw him walk. Okay, not saw, but every time I looked, he was in a different spot, so he must have."

"Why do you think he's here?"

"Dunno. He never said, I never asked. Some things just are. Maybe he was a wedding gift. That's when he turned up, isn't it? Day after our wedding?"

"Day after my kidnapping, you mean? But we moved. How did he find us? You didn't get him brought here, did you?"

"No. How could I? Look at him. He's bloody massive. Guess he really likes us, right?" He remained stoic.

"He needs a name." Phage stroked his thick arm and looked up at the beast of rock.

"What did Jen used to call him? Big Head, wasn't it?"

"Yes, but that's not nice."

"When he talks, he can tell us his name. Until then, he's just the massive sculpture in the garden." I finished the pizza then downed my wine. "Fancy an early night?" I said, grinning wickedly. "It is my birthday."

"Now that sounds perfect." Phage's horny smile wavered then fell. "Damn."

"What?"

"The kids. The girls. We can't, you know, with them all here. They'll be up and down the stairs all night messing around and playing."

"Then I've got an even better idea," I told her. With her eyebrows raised, I took my beautiful wife of twenty years by the hand and led her down the garden.

We reached Tyr's barn eventually and I unlocked the door. Tyr was out as I knew he would be, so I locked the door behind us, all sound of the outside world cut off, and wasted no time stripping off my clothes.

Phage laughed like a horny youngster—but about a million years older than my daughter, as that ain't ever gonna happen—as she removed her clothes too, and we stood there, naked, in a barn smelling of dragon, unabashed, proud of our firm yet damaged bodies. Both of us were a mess of scars and burns, and the odd gunshot wound, but I was definitely a lot worse than my wife. Whether that was because I was so much older, or because she was a damn sight better fighter, I wasn't sure, but deep down I knew. Phage was seriously hardcore, tough as they came, with powers that made her nigh on invincible. Her injuries were from early on in her Necronote career, some even before they began because of the way they brought up young witches in her mother's sisterhood.

I stood there, grinning, as Phage held eye contact then did her thing. First there was one naked Phage, then there were two. Then four, eight, and they all moved in close, eyes twinkling, as the only good thing about being the birthday boy descended on me.

"Happy birthday." Phage pecked me on the cheek then skipped up the land back to the house while I remained there, panting, knackered, and about as happy as any man in the whole world could ever be.

I got myself together, sorted my hair, then followed my wife up to the house where all was ominously quiet. Quiet eleven-year-olds is not something you want to hear on a sleepover when it's not even bedtime. And then it began. Incredibly loud, tinny music blasted from the living room, vibrated the windows, made my insides judder, and the man-mountain on the lawn bounce up and down. My worst nightmare had come to pass. It meant only one thing. They were ready to do karaoke.

In a panic, I decided I'd better go warn Mrs. O'Donnell. They made such a bloody racket, and although her house was quite a way from ours, the caterwauling was always so loud and so high-pitched, it would send her ducks into meltdown and she'd freak out like she did last time and come around with her shotgun.

And then I remembered that not only did I have a personal phone I could carry around the world with me, but there were multiple landlines in the house, and everyone else had a phone too, even my old neighbor.

So I called her up instead and warned her. She swore at me, like it was my fault, but promised she wouldn't arrive bearing arms, then swore a bit more, and said she'd go lock the geese in somewhere and wear her ear mufflers.

Sometimes modern life sure was easy.

It still sucked though.

The house vibrated as a gaggle of young girls sang, or should I say butchered, whatever the hell the song was. All I knew was the original couldn't have possibly been that bad.

New Rules

"Say goodbye to Jen for me," I told Phage as we stood by the gate.

"I will. Can't believe they're all still asleep."

"Judging by the racket they made until the early hours, my guess is they'll surface just in time for lunch. They had a good time though. Mind you, I miss the cuddles and the getting woken at seven by her jumping on our bed."

"Haha, me too. Didn't feel like it at the time, did it? The bed thing, not the cuddles."

Phage and I were stalling and we both knew it. I didn't want to leave, she didn't want me to either. However many times we did this, it always cut deep. This could genuinely be the last time we saw each other. I ached to wake Jen and hug her tight, tell her I loved her before I left, but maybe it was for the best not to. I felt panicked, almost ran back in and embarrassed her in front of her friends, but I controlled myself even though it was hard.

"Be safe. Come home to us soon. Woofer, you look after him." Phage rubbed Woofer's head and he nodded, knowing she couldn't understand if he spoke. "Good boy."

His tail wagged but he was nervous. This was new to him. Woofer stayed at home. He went on little outings with us, but never very far, as no car meant no epic trips. The whole big, bad, wide world awaited him, and it was a scary prospect for the middle-aged Lab who liked his morning nap, his afternoon nap, the evening one, before it was time for the main sleep at night.

"He'll protect me. And Tyr has already left. He'll catch us up soon. Don't forget to look after the animals, and tell Bernard I'm docking his feed because he smashed the swing, the utter dick. How the hell can a bloody unicorn think it's a good idea to let their foal try to get on a swing? A swing!"

"Because he loves his daughter, same as you. He sees Jen on it and... Yeah, he's a dick." Phage laughed. Such a beautiful laugh. "But Kayin is no foal now. She's bloody massive already."

"I know. Damn, the years fly by, don't they?"

"Quit stalling, mister." Phage kissed me and I squeezed her hard.

"See you soon. Might be a week, hopefully less."

"Ride safely, and don't forget. We're here waiting for you."

I nodded, then with no reason to dawdle any longer, I headed out into the unknown.

Woofer ran alongside, happy to tag along. I worried about him already. Just this once, I told myself. He could come this one time and that was it. His place was at home, taking it easy and enjoying life. Oblivious to the things that went on out here in a world that changed faster than I could manage to keep up with.

More than anything, I wanted him to retain his innocence. He knew what Phage and I did, he heard the stories, and the very tall ones from Tyr. But the reality was different. Woofer was an innocent in a world where very few could call themselves that with a straight face.

As I cycled sedately through Shrewsbury town, past leaning Tudor half-timbered buildings, smiling and waving at familiar faces, everyone happy when they saw Woofer, I marveled again at the human race's ability to adapt so rapidly.

Not so long ago the place was full of cars, buses, motorbikes, and the odd bicycle. Now there were zero cars, a bus once or twice a day, and no motorbikes. There were a lot of bicycles though. On a sweltering summer's day the likes of which I had never known, there were still plenty of shoppers. Locals thronged to buy fresh produce. Bread baked that day, meat, fish, vegetables, all the perishables that wouldn't store for long at home now the energy quotas had tightened and most couldn't run freezers.

There were also no lights in the buildings as it was a luxury, even with advanced low power options. Why waste it in the day when everyone could see anyway? It made total sense, so why just a few years ago were there streetlights on twenty-four hours a day, every building lit up like a Christmas tree, and office blocks gleaming in the night when empty?

We sure had done some stupid crap. Undoubtedly, we would again. I know I had loads of stupid left inside to purge.

There was plenty of bad too. The roads were awful. Maintenance had ground to a halt, so the weather chewed away at the surface and potholes got bigger. More accidents occurred as cyclists crumpled their wheels and flew off their bikes. But the death-toll from traffic accidents was at a record low, so there was that.

Travel in general was back to being under strict curfew. We all had zones; we were not to leave our immediate area. It was worrying. Things were close to totalitarian, but the country was cleaner, there was no rubbish littering the streets, and the air was clear, but it simply didn't feel right.

Everyone felt it. An offness about everything. Like it wasn't really necessary. Why couldn't we travel to see family and friends? Why couldn't we generate more power? Why wasn't there an alternative to coal or nuclear that could see everyone having whatever electricity they wanted? This was the modern age, after all.

Thank god for my solar and wind turbine. Even though the batteries were becoming flaky and the arrays past their best, we had it better than most, so I didn't complain. Much.

Shops were different too. Over the previous two years there had been drastic changes in the laws of production worldwide. Plastic became a bad word. There were no tiny plastic toys, no sweets or products in individual wrappers. No tat, in other words. Everything had to be recycled, re-used, or it wasn't produced. Utterly sensible, but I missed Cadbury's Cream Eggs and tins of Quality Street at Christmas. Don't even get me started on the banning of shampoo in bottles. I mean, c'mon!

But I liked that Ikea went bust. Although I was definitely in the minority on that one.

Speaking of clean air. This was another year, so another chance to inhale noxious fumes. Every cloud has a silver lining, even if it is carcinogenic. Lungs already tightening in anticipation, I pulled up outside Necrosmoke, Pam's slice of nicotine-soaked paradise. I scowled at the stupid bottles of juice arranged neatly in the window, and the endless variations on black boxes to atomize the mysterious liquids, and wondered how business was now batteries were no easy thing to get hold of. Guess the tech had improved, same as for most things. You could run a phone for weeks at a time now, same for most modern devices, if you could get hold of them.

I pushed on the door and the bell rang as I let Woofer enter first, then stepped into what used to be smoker's paradise, now was something different. Crap, is what I mean.

"Woofer smells melon. Is there melon?"

My excited pooch checked for food but was disappointed. He did the rounds, sniffing everything, then sat, waiting for Pam to appear.

We waited, and waited, then waited some more.

"Pam? Hello?"

No Pam.

"Yo, Pam? Whassup!?"

Pam appeared from the back, looking disheveled and lovely. She frowned. "Did you just do a whassup?"

"Yeah. What, aren't we doing that any more?"

"We were never doing that," she lectured. "Because it is lame, and about as out-of-date as your hairstyle."

I put a hand to my lovely, drool-inducing locks. "What's wrong with my hair?"

"Nothing, if you're happy with it like that, it's up to you."

"Damn, Pam, way to make a guy feel uncomfortable."

"Woofer like Soph's hair. Like big scruffy dog."

"Gee, not you too, Woofer. Now I'll have to cut it."

"What did he say? And hello, it's Woofer, is it?"

The idiot dog's tail thumped against the shiny floor. Woofer jumped up, put his paws on the counter, and panted.

"He said he loves my hair and I look very handsome indeed."

Pam leaned forward. I gulped as the impressive cleavage hung low and delicious, then Woofer, dirty dog that he was, craned forward and gave her an almighty lick right where just about every person who had ever walked into Necrosmoke desired to lick.

"Oh, haha, silly dog." Woofer wagged like an idiot, got all excited, and as Pam leaned low he slobbered all over her face while she laughed and patted his head. Some guys get all the breaks.

Pam moved back after Woofer got a bit too keen. I told him to go sit by the door and guard it, his first official duty on the road. He practically fell over himself to fulfill his role.

"So, what's up? What you doing? You look a bit, um..."

"Disheveled?" she asked happily, as she ran a hand through her long, tangled locks.

"Yeah. Happy, but harried."

"Oh, I'm not harried. I'm just—"

"Sexy as hell," said a solid looking woman with the most fantastic blond locks and a beautiful smile.

"You got that right," said Pam, laughing.

"Ah, I get it. Been up to no good in the back room, have you?"

"Nah, just checking the stock levels," said the woman.

"Yeah, we had to delve rather deep to the back to ensure everything was neatly stacked." Pam laughed uproariously.

"Um, I'm sure that means something rude, I just can't fathom what. And I'm not sure I want to know," I chuckled, happy to see Pam so upbeat. She'd had a tough few years since her dad decided to end it all as he was sick to the back teeth with notes and murder and not being able to drive his Audi whenever he wanted. Pam was a trooper, had carried on regardless, but her joie de vivre had dimmed for a while there.

"Never you mind," said Pam. "Jukel, this is Soph. Soph, meet Jukel. My new squeeze."

"Pleased to meet you, Soph." Jukel held out her hand and we shook.

"You too. That's Slovakian, right?"

"Sure is. Family comes from there, back in the day."

I looked from Pam to her new friend, then back again. Was I reading this right? Her right? I was sure of it, but you had to be careful.

"Yes, she's a Necro. Don't look so worried."

"Sorry, but I didn't want to say the wrong thing."

"Don't sweat it." Jukel waved it away. "And yes, it means dog. Yes, I can shift into a dog. No big deal, about the most common gift there is, apart from talking to animals and a bit of whispering."

"Well, I can do the animal bit, but no whispering. Not much of anything else."

"What, at your age? You can't tell me you don't have a few tricks up your sleeve to have made it this far. I've struggled through just over ninety years now, can't imagine what it's like to be such an old man. Haha." She punched me on the arm playfully—she had serious power behind her.

"Yeah, well, I muddle through."

"Soph's about as tough as they come," Pam told her. "A real hardnut. He's got the will to see it through. He's an OG."

"An og?" I asked, confused.

"Original gangster," offered Jukel. "You know, one of the first, like really old and past it." She punched me again. Damn it hurt.

"I like that. Original gangster. That's me. Anyway, please, please tell me you still have the good stuff, Pam, not this fruity crap."

"I know, right? What is wrong with people? Smoking fucking fruit. Twats," agreed Jukel.

"I like you. I like her, Pam."

"Good, because otherwise I'd be terribly upset and have to call it off."

"Just get me my tobacco."

"Can Woofer say hello now?" he whined from by the door.

"Sure, buddy, come say hello to Aunty Jukel." She smiled as she spoke to Woofer, and never one to need asking twice to have a fuss, the manic mutt bounded over and got more attention than was strictly deserved.

"Us hounds stick together," said Jukel, as she looked up and saw my frown.

"It's your bacteria-laden funeral."

Pam sorted me out with a nice haul and then it was time to get going for real. We said our goodbyes and left the two laughing women to whatever "stocktaking" they still had left to accomplish.

"Woofer like women," panted my faithful companion.

"Me too. Never forget, they're the best."

Into the Unknown

We were heading strictly north towards Liverpool. I cursed my misfortune for snagging such an out-of-the-way task.

When would we be extinct? Was that the plan? It wasn't likely. There had always been peaks and troughs over the centuries, but that didn't make our current situation any less stressful. We were wiping each other out in a sick game of Battle Royale. Squid Game for the "magical" community.

We sweated, we swore, we damaged our hearts, minds, bodies, and very souls to continue this fucking charade of a life, and all for what? To satisfy the desires of unknowns who had played with the gifted amongst us since the dawn of our time. The sisters, a.k.a. the witches, knew. They understood this was no novel approach to keeping us in check. This went back to when we scrawled pictures on cave walls. This was part of what, of who, we were. As they liked to say, the notes endured.

I hated them.

My dark thoughts were crowded out by the view before me. I was taking the longer, more scenic route as it stopped me from getting so glum, and what stretched before me was the reason for such a choice. Open road, high, unruly hedges, fields, rolling hills, and the sheer, unmatched beauty of the Shropshire countryside. Farmers cut early grass for silage. Sweetcorn, wheat, barley, and all manner of crops were being dragged, dug, cut, or uprooted from the parched earth. We still had a climate that would tolerate such farming, but for how long nobody knew. The forecasts were mixed. Some were convinced we'd be an arid desert in decades, others told of coming rains of biblical proportions as the worldwide weather patterns ran amok for a while before settling down to more stable post-environmental disaster levels and we'd all live happily ever after.

The world was still a mess. Weather was unpredictable like never before, and wet places were dry, and dry places wet. Cold places too warm, warm places too cold. Ice caps melted, frozen tundras and permafrost caused utter catastrophe as entire cities slipped into gaping wounds in the earth, and endless animals were on the verge of extinction. The seas were clearing year on year though, and record numbers of marine life had been recorded, and insect populations and bird numbers were better than ever.

So it was working, these barbaric universal policies, but we weren't out of the woods by a long stretch, if we ever would be.

There I went again, dour thoughts when I should be easing my mind with what lay right in front of my eyes.

"Come on, Woofer, let's rest up for a while and have some lunch. Where's Tyr? Haven't seen him yet."

Woofer looked knackered anyway, so a break would do us both good. We rode on a ways until we found a suitable spot with deep shade and plenty of green grass to delight in. I pulled over at a farm gate, undid the orange twine that's seemingly the only kind they use, then sneaked through, closed it after us, and headed for a fat copse of ancient woodland.

Deep under cover in delightful shade, we settled on a carpet of thick moss, reveling in the damp and the musty air of such an ancient, rare place. I knew it was important to do this, not only for the cool, but because once we hit Liverpool it was gonna be an urban fantasy fan's wet dream. Hardly a tree in sight, nothing but concrete and more concrete interspersed with brick and maybe more concrete if you were lucky. It was important to be grounded, to keep in mind this country was awesome, not depressing.

Woofer panted and spun in circles until he got comfortable, then plopped himself down and looked at me expectantly.

"You did good, boy. Well done. How're the legs? How's the hip?"

"Woofer tired. Legs tired. Hip good. Hungry."

"Me too." I fished about in my pack, then got out our sandwiches. I threw one to Woofer, bit into my own, then sorted out a bowl of dog food for him too. He'd need all his energy for this trip, so I'd worry about his diet and expanding bottom when we got home.

Not if. When. When we got home.

My dozing was interrupted by a familiar weight on my lap. I opened my eyes with a smile as my companion settled and turned his long neck to stare at me. Such strange eyes. Vertical slit iris, purple pupils, orange sclera, about as weird as weird can get. But not for a dragon.

"Where have you been, eh?"

"Tyr hunting," he said proudly. His chest puffed out and the spikes running along his spine twitched as he arched his back. Powerful muscles were now present.

"You look like you filled your belly. You want anything else?"

"Tyr not like man food now. You know this. Want fresh food. Want birds and bugs and meat."

"I know, just offering. Sleep a while, rest, then we can head off. Poor Woofer's knackered."

"Woofer need more exercise. Get strong like Tyr." With that, the growing dragon curled up in my lap and his eyes closed.

I studied him as he fell asleep. The rate of change was remarkable ever since he kind of chewed down on a guy and drank his blood. He had gone from approximately the size of an eagle four years ago to that of a dog. But the change in body shape was what was most intriguing. The horns swept back over his head ridge, hard as iron. His legs were powerful, bunched with knotty muscle, and the claws were dangerous as hell. He could crush rocks with them easily. His tail was fat and just as lethal, and his wings were like old leather.

Tyr now almost exclusively caught his own food, and delighted in fresh kills whenever possible. He had a true hunter's mindset. His chameleon-like abilities had improved somewhat, although he couldn't always control it. He still had a long way to go though, was a child, maturing like Jen did in leaps and bounds but nowhere near being an adult. Gone were the squeaky voice and childish antics. In its place was a push to become an adult, even though he believed himself to be one already. He liked to play a little, silly things delighted him, and yet he was becoming more unruly, disobedient, forging his own path. Again, just like young children do when they realize they have their own minds and don't have to always do as they are told.

In other words, he was growing up. I had ensured he and Jen spent a lot of time together to secure their bond. It was beyond important, as dragons were faithful to those they matured with, but would absolutely disregard anything told to them by anyone outside that circle. They were wild, free, dangerous creatures, and once he was fully grown, many years from now, and long after Jen was, he would be a true creature of magic. Gone for long stretches at a time to places we could never follow, learning, honing skills, able to understand the Necroverse in ways impossible for humans. With age would come great knowledge, and there was no doubt that a dragon grew to become far more intelligent than a human if given time.

But for now, he was still a wyrmling, and I felt the weight of responsibility deeply for ensuring he wasn't a danger to us all and would help my daughter when the need arose.

"Sleep well, my friend. Sleep well."

I pulled my hat down low and closed my eyes, just for a little while.

Long Slog

After a generous smoke and a little more to eat, it was time to hit the road again. I was out of sunscreen—there were production and thus quota problems—my hat made my head sweat, and having to wear a shirt and jeans to stop getting burned put me in a sullen, why me, mood. But I'd tried lightweight cotton and all it did was tear. Denim was the way to go, and it hid the bloodstains better.

Woofer was struggling too. He was used to cool interiors, food and water in plentiful supply, and his favorite thing besides having a fuss—sleep. Tyr was happy as only a dragon could be in an ever-warming environment. He reveled in his freedom, his newfound abilities, his skills and general dragon awesome sauce. But just like Woofer, he was a creature that spent much more time asleep than awake. I'd heard that the ancient dragons slept for years, even centuries, at a time if there was nothing much going on that interested them, and it didn't surprise me.

So Tyr alternated between brief flights and resting on the handlebars when the coast was clear, which was most of the time even on a main thoroughfare as everyone was so well spaced out. It did not make for an easy ride. I had to keep angling to the side so I could see. And the bugger kept ringing the bell.

Drones buzzed overhead, keeping tabs on the populace, ensuring rules were followed. Necrodrones too, watching me, a reminder my actions had consequences and there was no escaping my duty.

I'd had zero insights into the source of notes in the intervening four years since I got an inkling of something from a smug elf I'd banished back to his own land, and I was still unsure if it was a good thing or a bad thing.

Part of me wanted to know, but most of me didn't, as I understood that with knowledge came danger. For me, and for my family if it was ever discovered. But I couldn't help wondering. Who were they? What did they want? Was there even an end goal? Was it really to weed out the weak, the evil? Most of the people I had killed had been obviously damaged or went against the rules we all knew had to be obeyed, but there were always exceptions. Doubts. And some I knew were tests. You went to a location and you just knew you shouldn't hurt this person. So you didn't, even if they tried to kill you because they knew they'd been marked by a note.

But usually I killed them. I was good at it. One of the absolute best. And it hurt. So, so badly. I was a mess of contradictions and it pained me so deeply I wanted to cry, curl up in a ball and sleep and never surface. But I always carried on; something inside drove me forward.

I hated to admit it, but I did want answers. We all did. The thoughts scared me. What then? There was nothing to be done anyway. The notes endure. They have been here since the beginning. We are chosen. We are marked. We are not the masters of our own fate.

We are playthings.

But I was alive. And there is true beauty in the world. True happiness. Nobody had it all. I certainly didn't. But I knew one thing with absolute certainty: I had more than I deserved.

So I rode along an empty road, heading north to Liverpool to go and most likely kill a man for the sole reason that I didn't want to die.

How weak, how pathetic I was. But there was no alternative.

Through the afternoon heat, into the evening, I pushed hard, stopping for short breaks but never truly at rest. I felt rushed for some reason, as though this had to be done soonest. That all was not as it seemed and I would need the time. So I forged ahead, legs burning, some serious chafing going on, as the heat sucked me dry, the animals complained, and my head filled with question upon question that had reverberated around my head ever since I learned of the Necronotes when still a child. May my parents rot in hell for letting me know such things and ruining my childhood.

A Call Back

My phone rang and I wasted no time pulling over — I needed an excuse for a rest.

"Soph, is that you?" came the almost imperceptible whisper.

"Pam? Why are you whispering?" Something wasn't right here. I adjusted my phone and pulled my hair back from my ear.

"I'm in deep shit. Really deep. Can you come and help? Please?"

"What's happened? Where are you? What's the problem?"

"I'm at home, at the horse sanctuary. And I'm screwed. I'm in a barn, the big one with the bales. I'm cowering like a spineless amateur. Argh, aaah, oh, shit that hurts. Fuck, she got me good. Soph, please hurry. You know I wouldn't ask unless it was urgent. Really urgent. Damn, it's your bloody birthday, isn't it. Shit, sorry. I forgot. Well, it's been nice knowing you. Guess you're miles away, right?"

"Pam, just tell me what happened. I can get there if you really need me, but tell me what's going on. Are you safe?"

"For a while. Not long. Shit, I was thinking you were at home. Wouldn't take you long if you took Kayin. That bitch, my new squeeze, she's a fucking Necro."

"Yeah, I know that."

"No, aargh, damn that hurts bad, she got a note. With my name on it. She's a sneak, a pretender. She used me, Soph. She came here to fucking kill me. And she almost succeeded. Well, nice knowing you."

The line went dead. I stared at my phone; the connection was severed.

And everything was going so well too.

Pam was an old friend, a very old friend, and I liked her a lot. She was kind, generous, had breasts to make a guy's life that little bit better as you knew for a fact there were things worth living for, and she gave me tobacco and unicorns. But I was hours away. She'd be dead before I got there, wouldn't she? Could she last out that long being injured and somebody searching for her? That bloody snake, Jukel. That was a low move. But clever. You had to give her that. She'd insinuated herself and was biding her time, knowing she had seven days to fulfill her note.

What should I do?

I knew what I had to do, but that it was a bad move. I'd done it once before, so should be able to do it again. But it wasn't a good idea and I'd pay for it. What choice did I have? I would not let a friend down. Especially not Pam.

I called out to Tyr and he came immediately. Woofer was looking concerned so I scratched behind his ears, told him it was okay. He whined.

"Pam is in serious trouble. I have to go help her. I don't know how long I'll be, maybe a while. I might have to be away until tomorrow. God knows how I'll get back here, I might have to," I shuddered at the thought, "ask Bernard. Damn, what a mess. I'm going to morph, go help Pam, but it's a long way and it's hard, so you'll have to be patient and stay here. Both of you."

"Tyr can help."

"Woofer can come?"

"No, you both stay here. Tyr, the place is full of hay and straw and wooden buildings. I know you want to help, but it's too dangerous. There are lots of animals there. Woofer, you need to guard my bike. It's important. So wait here, do not stray, and I will be back as soon as I can. Understand? Tell me you both understand? This is important, guys."

"Woofer will stay, guard bike. Woofer is great guard dog."

"You sure are." I smiled at him and patted his head.

"Tyr guard sky. Tell Woofer if anyone comes."

"That's the spirit."

We moved to a secluded spot behind a hedge and I left the bike leaning into it. It wasn't perfect, and there was a chance of us being seen, but it would have to do.

"Right, let me get my pack then I'm outta here." I sorted out a few things into a smaller pack, stashed the larger one deep into the hedge, shrugged into my gear, checked my knife, took a deep breath, nodded to the animals, then gritted my teeth and was consumed by pain. Unbelievable, all-encompassing pain.

Everything was stripped from me. My body, my mind, my very soul. All that remained was lit nerves. I screamed into nothingness as I became motes of Soph. Billions of particles each carrying my makeup shot into the air and sped towards a distant destination. No thought, no guidance, just intent. I endured because I had no choice, and lifetimes later, when I believed I couldn't cope a moment longer, I snapped back into my body. Complete. Dressed, with my pack, already reaching for the comfort of the well-worn leather sheath and the blade it contained. A blade that had killed countless. A weapon imbued with the blood and spirits of numerous Necros.

I stood stock still while I came back to myself. Pain dissolved, leaving me an empty shell of anger, hunger, hurt, and worry for my friend. Yet there was also a smugness. A middle finger to the witches, wizards, and warlocks, those for whom such an act was casual. But the witches had told me nobody could travel such distances, never at such speeds. I had amazed them four years ago, and I amazed myself too. Maybe old Soph was pretty good at this magic business after all.

It was almost dark where I stood amidst bales of straw —bedding for the horses. The barn was huge and filled to the rafters. An open affair to let the air travel and stop the precious commodity from rotting. I was right in the middle of it, with towering walls of stubble all around me. A room within the barn. Why was it stored like this? Duh. Because Pam was smart and would always have plenty of hiding places, same as we all did. A just-in-case, because you never knew.

A low groan snapped me to attention. A dark form cramped against the sweet straw. I fumbled my way over in the gloom and crouched. I could smell the blood.

"Pam, it's me. How you doing?"

"Soph. You came. Haha, couldn't keep away, huh? Ugh, damn! She fucked me up good. Thank you. Thank you so much. I'm sorry, bet this is the last thing you need."

"Hush, it's fine. I was just having a fun bike ride. Nothing to worry about."

"I can't believe I fell for this. She played me like a child. Me! I'm too old for this crap."

"And exactly how old might that be?" I asked, smiling.

"Never you mind. Let's just say I'm not as old as you but I remember electricity being a thing."

"What happened? Where is she?"

"She's around somewhere. Close. But where, I don't know. She'll find me soon enough though. Can probably smell the blood. Shit, I'm screwed. Soph, I'm sorry. You should go. I don't want to put you in danger. I didn't know what to do, who else to call. I panicked. Go, don't worry. This was a bad idea. Selfish."

"Don't be daft. We're friends. I'll sort it. So, what happened?"

"She did a fucking number on me. We were going to have dinner. I came out to check on the animals and then I turned around and bam, she fucking stabbed me. I kicked her arse, but my side was all messed up. She was down and

I figured I'd got the better of her, but I was stupid, got my pride hurt. So I made her tell me what she was playing at. She fooled me, planned it. Wanted to make it easy for herself. Get me off guard then slip the knife in. Such an amateur. How could I fall for this?"

"Because we don't play dirty like that. It's sneaky and low and we don't treat people that way. How could she do that after getting to know you? That's one cold bitch."

"She shared my bed, Soph. I liked her. I bloody well cooked for her, and you know what I'm like in the kitchen."

"Crap," I offered helpfully.

"Haha. Yeah, utter crap. I liked her, I really did."

"I know. She seemed nice. But hush now, let me see." I got out my phone and pulled a lightweight jacket from my pack then draped it over my head and fumbled around to find Pam's wound.

"That ain't the right bit, mister."

"Oops. Sorry." I found her ribs and her right side then lay almost flat on the straw and turned on the light. The wound was was red, raw, and oozing. Her vest was in tatters. There were bite marks across her trim belly, and multiple puncture wounds from teeth.

"Wow, she got nasty, huh?"

"I should have killed her straight away, but I wanted to know. She told me, then she turned. A bloody dog! A lovely Golden Retriever. She launched. She's got some weight behind her. Fuck! Almost got me, then I slashed her good on the flank and she went down so I ran away and hid like a scared girl."

"Okay, that's enough. Just lay still and I'll wrap you up. No screaming," I warned. Pam tensed as I poured iodine over her belly and side then bandaged her tight. It would have to do for now. Pam held in her screams as I got her into the jacket; she was shivering despite the heat.

"Thanks, and sorry."

"Don't sweat it. But you owe me a pouch."

"Hey, if I survive this, you get to smoke for free. Although, I did give you a unicorn. Argh, hell, hurts like a bitch."

"I'm gonna be around a long time," I warned her.

"I hope I am too. Goddamn!" hissed Pam. "This hurts like a mo-fo."

"Is that what the kids say?" I asked.

"Yeah, get with the times, old man." Pam laughed weakly and I knew she was in a bad way.

"Okay, so, what does she look like again? What kind of dog?" I wasn't paying enough attention. The morph still had me unsettled and I needed to focus.

"A bloody Golden Retriever. Lovely. She's quick, and she's tough, and bloody brutal."

"Stay here. I'll be back soon."

I grabbed my gun, much as I hated the things and hardly ever even used it, stuffed it into my belt, secured my pack, then carefully clambered out of the maze of bales and into the relative light of the yard.

Pam had a fast-running stream running through her property so generated plenty of power, which meant the stables were lit and so was the yard, casting long shadows with plenty of places to hide. But Jukel didn't know I was here, and would be confident. I wandered over to the stables, warning the horses I was coming, and I asked them to be silent as their mistress was in danger. They understood, and filled my mind with worry. They knew something was going on and many had tried to kick the doors down, but they did as asked and remained calm.

I reached out to them all, asked what they knew, and got a little information but not enough. I was guided to where Jukel had done her animorph act. Socks, boots, jeans, pants, and vest lay in a heap, so either she was still in animal form or wasn't bothered about her modesty. She wouldn't be; Pam had already seen it all.

A trail of blood ran along the front of the stalls then vanished as Jukel had headed off on her search. I kept to the shadows, knife out, and began my unexpected hunt.

I didn't have long to wait as a voice called out, "Where are you, lover? I'm sorry, Pam. I know this is low, but what choice do I have? It's you or me, and I like being me. Come on, let's get this over with."

I followed the voice and there she was, standing in the yard, naked and fierce looking. She had a nasty cut on her side, thanks to Pam, and it was bleeding, but it clearly wasn't that deep or serious. Jukel was filthy, her hair was wild, her actions nervous and manic as she turned this way then that, listening for the slightest sound.

I hesitated, and I never hesitated. I could get her easy. A quick morph, a slit of her throat, and it would be done. Pam would be saved. I could get her the help she needed, then return to my business. But I paused.

So many killings, so much death, so much foulness, but I had never, ever killed a woman before. Men killed men, women killed women. It was the way of things. Stupid. Should it matter? I believed it should. Because it wasn't a fair fight? No. Many women made me seem like an amateur. Were stronger, faster, had more gifts, and were certainly much smarter, but it was how I was wired. Deep beliefs from a bygone age, when men were men and women were protected, cosseted, and didn't fight. It was all a lie of course. Some had been treated badly, as second-class citizens even though everyone knew they were the backbone of society, did the most important job in the world.

But there was a difference. There simply was. You did not hit women, you did not mistreat women, you most certainly did not murder women.

There was no alternative. She would destroy Pam. That wasn't going to happen.

I became dust and raced towards the woman that would murder my friend.

Stupid Apology

"Sorry," I whispered, as I swiped right to slit Jukel's throat. Willing, and able, to put an end to this woman's life, much as it felt wrong.

I got nothing but air.

The blond, shaggy dog turned and launched before I had a chance to acknowledge what an utter dick I was for apologizing.

Her surprising weight knocked me back and I stumbled whilst slashing haphazardly with the knife, hot with anger and a little shame mixed in for good measure. Jukel snapped down anywhere she could, a flurry of wildness both impressive and disconcerting.

I yanked fur, and rolled, hoping to use my own bodyweight to pin her down, but she tore at my shirt, getting cloth and flesh, then was free. I morphed again, came back to true form behind her, and booted her as hard as I could in the belly. Shame filled me as the dog yowled pitifully but came at me without pause, fangs bared, eyes wild. Scared, but full of intent.

I morphed again, really pushing my limits, solidifying at a distance, then pulled the gun and fired off three rounds. The sound was deafening. I hated these bloody things, and the dog was either very fast or I was suddenly a crap shot, as the bullets kicked up shards of concrete. The horses went wild in the stalls and I had zero opportunity to talk them down.

With amazing grace and speed for such a large dog, Jukel came at me hard and fast. No time to think, I jabbed at the animal as it went for my legs. But I was using my left hand to punch out with the knife, and my coordination was for crap, so the wounds were superficial. She locked onto my shin, but I stabbed again and again, hitting flesh and bone. I kicked out and she was shaken off, howling in pain. The dog stepped back warily, shook out from head to tail, then lowered her head as she snarled viciously, body low to the ground.

"Pretty low, treating Pam like that. Beyond callous."

Jukel shifted into human form. Bones creaked and flesh made weird sounds as she cricked her back and stood upright. Her body was a mess now. Covered in cuts, bruises, open wounds, many bleeding freely. She spat blood as she pulled clumps of knotted hair from her eyes. Jukel glared at me, half lost to the bloodlust. Uncharacteristically, I wasn't that far gone. I wished I was, because it hurt to feel like this. Being confronted with what I had done, and knowing what I would do, was not a nice feeling. Unable to hide behind the veil of violence-induced madness.

I was here, I was aware, I accepted the foul deed I was about to commit.

"I'm sorry, okay," she cried, hands out in supplication. "I figured I'd make friends, then finish her off before she knew anything. I like her, god help me. I think Pam's great. I let it go too far. Couldn't help myself. Even though I knew what I had to do, I really like her." Jukel took a deep breath —a rattle came from her chest and I knew she was as good as dead—then shouted, "I'm sorry, Pam. Truly I am."

"You should have played fair."

"Fair!? Fucking fair! This shit is anything but fair. How do you think I feel? I had to kill this lovely woman because it says so on a note. And why? What has Pam ever done?"

I frowned. She had a good point. Why Pam? Pam kept to herself, did nothing but good. Never hurt anyone apart from her marks. "Nothing. She's a great person."

"Exactly. And me, I'm not worthy of her. But I have to do it. Had to, haha. It's so hard, you know that. I made a mistake, shouldn't have tried this, but it was too late and I didn't know what else to do. So yeah, I tried to kill her. It was her or me. Why is this happening?" she screamed to the sky. To our silent observers.

"I'm sorry too." I raised the gun and took aim. Jukel stood there, panting, resolute. She wouldn't run, wouldn't attack. She knew this had to end now.

The clatter of horse hooves on concrete broke my focus. A powerful, midnight-black giant of a mare with a flowing mane thundered towards Jukel. She opened her arms wide and laughed, head back, as the horse smashed into her stout, ravaged body and knocked her to the ground. The mare snorted as it skidded to a halt. It turned fast then trotted back to the mangled form. The impressive creature had a large gash on its side and multiple smaller wounds.

For several seconds there was an absolute stillness. Like the world had been put on pause. We both stared at the ruined body of a woman lying in the yard; her skin was so pale under the icy lights. Blood sparkled as the body convulsed then was still. The horse paused mid-movement, as if thinking, then shook out its glistening mane and reared up on hind legs as it whinnied. Decision made, it stomped down with all its weight onto Jukel's head. The skull split open. Blood and brain splattered the yard. Jukel's corpse spasmed, limbs twisting like a puppet performing its final act before the strings were cut. She soiled herself, then all was still. Not a sound.

The animals in the stalls ceased their calls and kicking as all heads turned to Pam. The mare stood there, looking down at the corpse, breathing hard through its nose, then the change began. The mighty creature shrank, and as Pam came back to herself, she dropped onto torn knees beside the body and wailed.

Pam wept for her own sins, for mine, and for Jukel's. For the things we were made to do, for the despicable tricks we played on each other, the violence we were capable of and had carried out, and for the sick, twisted games we clung to because we wanted to save our own skin.

I ran over to her, yanked off my shirt and covered her nakedness a little, then helped her get unsteadily to her feet and guided her away from the sight before us.

There was no glory in this, no victor. There never was. Just another dead Necro, our world a little more broken, our minds and hearts corrupted once again.

Look what we'd become. Look what we did to each other.

There had to be a way out from this. There was no way out of this.

Damsel in Distress

I helped Pam limp back to her cottage. She was sweating badly, already burning up, and swearing like me on a good day because of it. But mostly she was just defeated. Broken by the betrayal, by being marked in the first place. I sensed the emotions vying for supremacy. The doubts, the worries, the anger.

But mostly the deceit.

Physical injury is visceral, raw, and almost unbelievably painful. Until you've experienced life-threatening wounds, you can't even imagine the agony the human body is capable of experiencing. Having your heart broken hurts way more. Knife cuts heal faster than emotional tears.

"Come on, nearly there," I told her, as she hobbled through the front door and I closed then locked it behind us. A tiny horse not much larger than Woofer bounded down the flagstone hallway and whinnied noisily. It shook its head side-to-side and nudged Pam insistently until she reached out a hand and rubbed his mane.

"It's okay, boy, nothing to worry about. I'm alright. Sorry to leave you locked in."

"Is Pam really okay?" asked the horse.

"Um, she's in a bad way, but it isn't fatal. Don't worry, we'll get her fixed up."

"That woman, she did this?"

"She sure did. Um, but she's dead."

"Good." The pint-sized stallion rubbed its head against Pam but she yelped.

"Be careful there, buddy. She's hurt bad."

"Sorry. Pam will live?"

"Yeah, she'll live. It will take more than that to beat her."

"What's he saying?" gasped Pam.

"Just asking how you are. Come on, let's get you sorted out. And put some damn clothes on, woman, you'll give me a heart attack staring at your arse. Damn, Pam, it's not even possible to have a bottom as perfect as that. It's a crime against wobble. Too pert. Not to mention the beauties you have up front." I think I blushed. I'd never been so familiar with Pam, wouldn't dream of it, but everything felt different now, like we were true buddies and I could joke about such things.

Pam glared at me. I swallowed. Guess I got that wrong. Then she smiled, and said, "They are fucking awesome, right?" and jiggled. She gasped in pain.

"Ha, serves you right! Women the world over will be shouting, 'In your face, Pam, for being so damn cocky about gifts you had no part in making.' So hold still."

"It's not the making that's key. It's the maintaining."
Pam winced.

"Okay, let's do this. Sorry, but you need to get cleaned up. Got a shower downstairs?"

"No. It's up there." Pam pointed up the carpeted stairs.

"Right, that's a problem. But you have to get cleaned, then we can sort the wounds out. You up for this?"

"Not like this. Look away."

"You can't turn into a bloody horse in the house! Get serious. You were massive."

"Yeah, I know. Just wait. It's actually easier like this."

I averted my gaze as instructed, and when the cracking stopped I looked. Pam was roughly the size of the horse beside her. Wasting no time, she traversed the stairs in a rather comical manner, then collapsed at the top and became human again.

I grabbed my shirt then rushed up and helped her get to her feet. "Impressive."

"Yeah, it comes in handy for such occasions. Takes less out of me, conservation of energy and all that. Damn, I am so hungry. I'm wasting away here."

With her arm hitched over my shoulder, I helped her along the landing until we got to the bathroom. Inside, I ran the shower and, ignoring the usual urges, inspected Pam from head-to-toe to get a grip on what needed to be done. She really was wasting away. The energy needed to shift into such a large animal must be astronomical, and she had lost pounds in weight. It could become dangerous if she didn't get food into her, and fast.

Shifting like that was not easy, and it could kill you, especially in heightened emotional states, so we had one more problem to add to the list.

"Just sit on the loo while I get some food."

I slid into my bloodied shirt then ran downstairs, told the tiny pony all was well, went into her country style kitchen and grabbed bread and meat slices, slapped them together, then dashed back up.

Pam snatched the food and stuffed it in with utmost urgency. I did likewise. She was definitely hungrier, but I was so starving I couldn't think straight. We ate, we sighed, we groaned.

Once she'd had her fill, I helped her up and got her into the shower. She said she'd be okay, so I left her to it and waited outside the door. She was fast, probably because she was hardly able to stand. I gave her a towel, and once she was wrapped up I found the meds where she directed before helping her into the bedroom.

The bed was unmade, and it smelled of perfume. Hers and Jukel's. I pulled the cover back over and plumped up the pillows. Pam lay down gratefully.

She gritted her teeth and closed her eyes. Pam didn't cry. I did. For her, for Jukel, for me. For all of us. She opened her eyes as I wiped my face.

"You big soft bugger," she laughed.

"Got some grit in them. Come on, let's sort this mess out."

I spent the next hour cleaning and disinfecting her wounds, stitching her up after several injections to numb the localized pain, and then dressed and bandaged the wounds as best I could. I was no pro, but it wasn't too sloppy either. Practice makes perfect. I wasn't perfect, but I'd had a lot of practice.

"There, finished," I said, standing to admire my handiwork. All the adrenaline had faded by now, and as I stared down at Pam, bandaged and bruised, like she was about to go out hot trick or treating, I think we both realized it was a rather awkward moment. I tried not to take in the sight of Pam, naked and awesome, defenseless and ravishing, lying spread-eagled on the bed, but I was a man, and she was, well, she was there. That's about all it takes really.

"Thanks, and I mean it. Now fuck off out of my room, you dirty old bugger." Pam grinned. She'd live.

I saluted crisply, snapped my heels together, then went to cool off.

Bloody Jukel, bloody notes, bloody life. Ugh, how could they do this to Pam? She was wonderful. A truly nice person.

Wasn't she?

I wandered back to the kitchen and rummaged about, then made beans on toast with three fried eggs each, coffee, and opened a bottle of wine from the warm fridge—it was probably broken, and it wasn't easy to get replacements. Once I'd set it all out, I called up to Pam.

I heard her banging about and using some very creative swear words, but left her to it as that was the kind of gal Pam was, then opened the front door to get some air and basically feel like I was doing something useful. Not that I was. At all.

Visions of bloodied boobs and naked thighs were absolutely not appropriate, so I most definitely did not think about that, so not having to eradicate such improper thoughts, I figured I should check on things in the yard, just in case. Why? No idea. Just a feeling.

As I dodged the horse shit and rubbed at my side—I'd forgotten I was hurt too—a familiar buzzing came from overhead. The drone came down low into the yard, hovered in front of me, probably reading my features and other esoteric tech things, then rose and continued towards the corpse. I followed, intrigued.

It glided almost on the ground, then juddered as if someone had lost the controls, before it rose up high and shot off.

No sooner had it done so, than what can only be described as a hole, because that's exactly what it was, opened above the corpse. A black pit of nothingness. I ran forward, unable to stop myself, then skidded onto my side, rolled onto my back, and peered up into the hole. It wasn't black underneath, it was a roaring inferno. Like the inside of a volcano. Lava spewed up, or down—the view of looking down into something but me looking up messed with my head—and then I rolled aside as it sank low until it covered Jukel.

I jumped to my feet, stared at the top of the hole, nothing but blackness, then it winked out of existence. Jukel, the gore, everything, was gone.

What about her stuff? I ran back in time to see a smaller hole descend, suck up her clothes, and wink out.

So that's how they did it. Another tiny piece of an impossible puzzle. Maybe one day they'd all fit together and I'd be the only Necro on the planet who knew how this bloody game worked. Or more likely, they'd send someone like me to kill me.

Dazed, and finally feeling the hurt of my wounds, I drifted back into the house and closed the door again.

"Awesome eggs," shouted Pam.

I locked us in. "How'd you know it was me?" I asked, as I wandered into the kitchen.

"I can smell you. Go get a shower. But eat your supper first. You look terrible."

"Come to think of it, I feel terrible."

Pam spat out beans and eggs as she laughed. I joined her. What else could I do? I'd already done my crying.

When we'd finished, I cleaned up the kitchen, helped Pam into the living room, and poured us more wine.

"Let's have a chat," said Pam, wincing as she tried to get comfortable on the sofa.

"Okay," I said warily, leaning against the door frame as I felt too exposed sitting down.

"Why do you think they targeted me?"

"I have no idea. You're great. And I mean that."

"I know. Utterly awesome." Pam grinned, a little manically, but it was understandable.

"Meds kicking in, are they?" I laughed.

"No, but I wish there were. Hurts like hell. But seriously, why me? Not to toot my own horn, but I'm not a bad person. I keep out of trouble, I look after the horses, run the shop, that's it. I don't get it. And what now? Another Necro tomorrow, and on and on until you can't be bothered to come save me anymore?"

"I'll always come, you know that."

"I'm so sorry about this. Were you in the middle of something?"

"About to be, but it can wait. I'll leave in a bit. Damn, no bike. Got a spare?"

"Of course. But you could take one of the horses."

"Thanks, but no. I'll need to take too much, and it never works out. Either too slow, too uncomfortable, or they throw me off. Bikes don't talk back, either."

"No, but they're slower, and knackering. You aren't in any state to cycle. You got hurt, and you're exhausted."

"Yeah, I am pretty beat. Let me think on it. First, let's solve your problems. Why was Pam marked? And what the hell was that out there just then?" I mused, not really thinking about what I was saying.

"What? Where?"

"No, nothing." I waved it away.

"Come on, what? Did you see something? Soph, they targeted me. No point worrying about secrets now."

"Of course there is. I saw how they take the bodies, that's all. The drone came, it looked at me, then there was this thing. A doorway. A rift. You know, reality splitting, like how elves and other Necros go back to their realms. Nothing really."

"I know shit all about that stuff. I always tell you, I just sell tobacco, look after the horses, go and kill someone once a year. I keep a low profile. I'm not into any of that like you are."

"Was," I reminded her. "I used to be pretty wild," I admitted. "Pushing the boundaries. And what did I get for my troubles? A bloody insane dwarf in the basement, a freak in the pub cellar, a troll in the garden, too many unicorns, endless paranormal creatures in the zoo, and a bloody big headache. You do the right thing. Stay out of it all."

"I wish I hadn't. It sounds exciting."

"Yeah, and exhausting. Look, it was nothing, but maybe not. I don't know why they let me see. It was weird. I mean, you ever hear of anyone witnessing how they dispose of bodies?" Pam shook her head. "Exactly. It was like they wanted me to see. But that's enough of that. I don't want you getting into trouble."

"I'm already in trouble, don't you see? I wonder if those I killed were like me? Nothing to hide, being good girls, then wham. You're dead. No explanation."

"I don't think so. Every person I've killed, there was a reason. A good one, I'm sure."

"Hundred percent?"

"No, not even close."

"So, I ask again. Why me? It's meant to be to stop the wild ones, the cruel, the unhinged, the dangerous. Those who won't play the game, keep it hush-hush, or dig too deep and try to uncover the truth. But now you're telling me you think they're trying to let you find out? That makes you dangerous."

"Yeah, this is what I'm afraid of. I don't want to know, Pam. I really don't. I want to stay alive. I have to. But..."

Pam eased herself forward. "But what?"

"What if this wasn't about you? What if they set it up? So you'd call for help? For me? So they could screw with me some more?"

"That's a pretty big leap of faith. One, they wouldn't know I'd call. Two, Jukel could have killed me earlier. Three, I could have killed her. Four, um, there probably is a four. Nah, you're letting your macho uber manliness go to your head."

"I'm not macho. Just a guy."

"Soph, I hate to break it to you, buddy, but you are about as manly as they come. Women swoon just being near you. You have this thing about you. An aura. Tough guy with a heart. Ladies lap that shit up. Not me, but the straight ones."

"Now that is a compliment. Never thought of myself like that. I know I'm tough when I have to be. That I have this thing inside that keeps me alive, but we all have that."

"No, we don't. Not like you. You don't hesitate, you act."

"I didn't today. I'm sorry, I almost let her win. I've never killed a woman before."

"And I've only killed ten men." She laughed, but I don't think it was a joke. "But trust me, you are a prize. As long as you like them grumpy, that is. And wrinkly. And you know, the hair thing you've got going on."

"Speaking of wrinkly," came the voice of a true angel.

"Phage, you're here. What? How? Why?"

"Tyr came and told me what you were doing. I figured you might need some help. Well, that Pam might. Hi, Pam. Damn, what happened?" Phage pecked me on the cheek, put a hand to my face, then stepped into the living room.

"I got my name put on a note. You didn't have to come. I already messed Soph about. I don't want to be trouble for you too. And I am sorry, Soph, I shouldn't have called."

"Of course you should have. Right, love?"

"Yes. We're friends," said Phage. "So, tell me what happened. And I mean all of it."

Pam and I filled in Phage, but I wasn't happy about her being here. Not happy at all. I guess it was obvious, as once Phage was up to speed, she turned to me and said, "Stop being so grumpy. I'm here because I thought you both might need me. This isn't our notes that we have to keep private. This is one of our own being marked, and we are allowed to help in any way we can. That's how it works."

"I know, but it could have been dangerous. We shouldn't be together like this for long. You know that. What if we both got killed? What about Jen?"

"I know, but I panicked. I worried. It's hard enough when you leave, when you left us this morning. But hearing you were back, and there was something I could do for a change, well, I had to come. You understand, right?"

"Of course," said Pam. "But he's right. I truly appreciate it, but it was a big risk."

"I can take care of myself. Don't worry about me."

"I worry about you every day," I told her.

"And I worry about you. So we're even. Now, are you gonna hog that wine or share?"

I went to get a glass for my fearless wife.

Infinite Possibilities

"Okay, I have to ask, even though there's other things to talk about," said Pam. "Phage, how did you know we were here? You said Tyr told you, but, um, you can't talk to the animals, can you? Am I wrong?"

"Yeah, she's right. Damn, I hadn't even thought about that. What's up?" I asked. "You getting new skills?"

Phage's neck flushed. "I wish. He, er, he came and woke me up. I was dozing in the living room and he tapped on the window. Scared me half to death. I realized it was him and went outside."

"To see a dragon in the dark. Braver than me," whistled Pam.

"It's only Tyr," shrugged Phage. "Anyway, he had a piece of Soph's shirt, and I panicked, thinking he was dead or something. I asked Tyr if he was and he shook his head. I asked him what was wrong and he, well, he danced about and I didn't have a clue what he was trying to say."

"Should have got him to write it down," I told her.

"Don't get smart," Phage laughed. "Anyway, I thought about it, then asked him questions, did some mimes, and we got there in the end."

"Okay, now I'm really intrigued," said Pam.

"Me too. What mimes did you do? Charades with a dragon; that's a new one on me."

We all smiled. We needed something like this to lighten the mood.

"It was beyond frustrating. I knew he was talking to me, that weird growl he does now his voice has broken, it was so strange. I asked if you were hurt, if you were close, things like that. I got as far as that but then drew a blank. But then Tyr blew smoke. Did you know he could do that?"

"No. He can breathe fire, and usually there's smoke after, but I've never seen him just breathe smoke."

"It clicked then. I asked if he meant you were smoking. He shook his head. Then I, er..." Phage flushed again.

"What? Come on, the suspense is killing us," laughed Pam.

"Okay, but bear in mind I was in a panic and worried and talking to a dragon."

"This is gonna be good, I just know it." I smiled at my wife; she scowled at me.

"Fine. I did this." Phage cupped her breasts then pulled her hands out as if showing they had grown considerably.

Pam and I burst out laughing.

"And he got that?" asked Pam.

"Straight away," said a flustered Phage. "He nodded his head. I asked if you were with Pam, and he said yes. It didn't take long to figure out you were here and there was a problem. So I came to help."

"Well, haha, thank you," said Pam. "I'm glad you came. I appreciate the help."

"My pleasure. Now, can we please change the subject?"

We sat around drinking, and chatting about this and that just to fill the silence, skirting the one topic we all wanted to talk about, as usual. Then, out of the blue, Phage blurted, "How old are you, Pam?"

"Blimey, where'd that come from?" Pam laughed.

"I just wondered. You know how old this grumpy bugger is, and how old I am, right?" Pam nodded. "I wanted some feedback, so I wondered."

"I'm over a hundred, less than two. That close enough?"

"Sure. And how did you decide? You know, what age to stay at? I need to make a decision. I don't want to be an old crone like some of the really strong witches. And some not-so-old, actually." Phage frowned. "So, I need to decide when to properly call it a day."

"I told you, you're fine whatever you decide." I said.

"What a charmer," said Pam. "Men. All idiots. Okay, Phage, I figured it best to basically halt it looking mid-thirties. It still creeps up on you, as you know. I think since I picked the cutoff point, I've aged a couple of years. I don't want to look old, as there's no getting younger, is there? I like being firm and supple and young, so why screw with a good thing?"

"That's what I figured. I slowed myself right down too. I guess I look a little older than you, but I don't want to look older than this. My mother is ancient, yet looks like an older sister. But some of the witches go right into old age before messing with anything. They like being crones. Don't worry, Soph, I'm not doing that, but it is getting awkward."

"I know what you mean," I told her. "Bloody parents and whatnot at school. People have already commented, how come we don't seem to be getting any older. It's awkward to be sure, and in a few years it will be impossible to hide."

"You just have to wait for them to all die then," said Pam.

"Seriously, how did you handle it?" asked Phage. "Soph just moves, starts again, and that's all well and good if there are no children, but you can't do that to kids. I don't want to move, either. I like it where I am."

"You just have to have no friends. It's what I do." Pam wasn't joking. This was a real ordeal and there was no easy answer.

I cleared my throat and gave my opinion, not that it was new to Phage. "You know how I've managed. I like this apparent age, and it has crept forward a little, same as it does for everyone, but yeah, it's an issue. We either drop out entirely like your mother and her cronies, or we move now and then and start over. The other option is to just wait it out. Do nothing, let everyone else get older and see what happens. But you know how that plays out. I've been chased out of towns in the distant past, typical hounded-by-an-angry-mob scenario, so that's not a good option. We have a while, but in ten years tops we have to start over."

"But there must be another way," insisted Phage. "Pam, you ever hear of one?"

"The only other option is what the witches know. You get a shroud, learn the whispers, make it appear like you're older. But even then, you gotta die sometime, right? You can't be an old lady for hundreds of years. No, Soph's right. If you mix with regular people you have to move. Or, and it's what I did once, you get killed and take over where the old you left off."

"Oh, yes, I've heard of that," said Phage, sitting forward and eyeing Pam greedily for more info.

"It's not a good idea," I told her. "Pam, how'd that work out?"

"A bloody nightmare. I came back as a slightly different me, but you can't hide these." She grabbed her chest, wincing. "And I was only slightly different. People kinda believed, but I got so many weird looks, and impossible questions. People didn't trust me. It was a mess. So I jacked it in and moved here. Opened up shop."

"And you've already been here too long," I told her.

"Don't remind me. But I like it here. I don't want to start again. I'm not going anywhere this time. I'm staying put."

"You can't," I told her.

"Just watch me." Pam was resolute, but I knew it wouldn't last. It was our cross to bear. We did not age unless we chose to, and who would choose old age over staying young? The end result would be the same anyway. You'd hang around as an old duffer for centuries and that's the same as being young for centuries. No, you moved, started again, maybe got a slight face change by the witches, and hoped you never bumped into anyone you used to know.

"So there's no solution?" Phage was clearly disappointed, but we'd had this conversation multiple times, and she knew the score from the witches too. Can't blame her for trying though.

"I told you." I poured the last of the wine, wincing as I bent.

"How you doing?" asked Phage.

"Fine. I need to get cleaned up though. I'll sort it after my wine. So, what does the future have in store? You going to go all wrinkly or do we move?"

"Let's see when the time comes. I wish there was another way."

"You know that there is, right?" said Pam, looking smug and cryptic as hell.

"Don't you dare," I warned. "I am not going down that rabbit hole. Come on, Pam, you ever even hear of anyone doing it?"

"Yes, I have as a matter of fact. And so have you. It's just you never hear how they got on, because you can't. You should tell her, at least. So she knows all the options."

"It's bull, and even if it isn't, then no way. Too freaky. Messes with your head and you won't know until you arrive if it even works. Hell, you could wind up anywhere, any time, living with your bloody mother-in-law or something."

"Will you please tell me what you're both on about?" shouted Phage.

"Multiple universes," I said, shuddering.

"It's what all the kids are doing these days," said Pam, with a wink. "You know there are multiple, infinite universes, right?"

"People say there are, but it makes no difference, as we have ours."

"We do," agreed Pam. "But there are universes out there where, say, you guys have vanished. Got killed, walked off a cliff, or are even still alive. You go into that other version of events, and you either just step into the space you've left, or you, you know, you kill yourselves and take over. Best part is, you do it to your younger selves, and then you have a good load of years before you catch up and anyone asks any questions. You just use some good make-up or plastic surgery or get the witches to change you, so you look younger and can live happily for many years."

"In an alternate version of the world," I reminded her.

"Hey, I never said it was perfect."

"That sounds horrible. Everything would be different. Wouldn't it?'

"Not if you picked the right one. It would be like this world, just with a gap you can slot into. Okay, I'm beat. I need more painkillers, I need my bed, and I need to say thank you once again, Soph. And to you, Pam. Thanks for coming. And so fast too. Hey, how did you get here so quick?"

"I was going to morph then thought Soph would need transport. So I, er..."

"Oh, no, you didn't?" My heart sank.

"Had no choice. And to be fair, he was super fast and hardly moaned at all."

"And now he's going back home with you," I told her.

"You can't morph again. Look at you, you're a wreck. You need him, and you need his speed. You need his help."

"I do not. Absolutely no chance. I'd rather walk."

"Hey, guys, what are you talking about?"

"Bernard!" we both blurted.

Wait for it. Wait for it.

CRASH!

"Did somebody call?"

"Oh, for fuck's sake, Bernard. It's not a hole, it's a bloody window!" I smiled, just because, you know, I loved cleaning up glass and doing a spot of glazing of an evening whilst half-pissed and stressing about my future, or lack of.

It was the middle of the night by the time Phage and I had sorted Pam out with fresh dressing, more meds, a ton more food for all of us, and I'd fixed up the window with some ply. Pam would have to get a glazier, as numpty the unicorn had messed up the frame too. I was handy, but not that handy.

I showered, changed my shirt, scowled at the haunted face in the mirror, then nodded to myself. Survive, Soph, just keep on surviving. But, oh, how I wanted to weep. When would this nightmare be over? How much more could I take? Was I even human? I felt like a monster. A broken, scarred, irrevocably damaged monster. Knowing I had to be brave for those I loved, I turned away from my reflection and went back downstairs.

With Pam tucked up in bed, snoring soundly, it was just Phage and I in the quiet house. Plus the sleeping horse. There were no words left, so we held each other for a while and then Phage left. Jen was home alone, hopefully still asleep, and Phage had written a message and left a phone beside her bed, but it still wasn't a good move. She had to have someone there. There was always a just-in-case with our lives, so she morphed back, knowing she could rest up once sure Jen was safe.

That left me, one stupid unicorn, and my note, still unfulfilled, with a night lost. Days remained, but my mood was dour as I got my gear together and a few choice items raided from Pam's pantry.

Leaving Pam like this didn't sit well, but Phage had said she would check in, and come help out if needed. A doctor would arrive and treat her wounds properly in the morning—we had people we could rely on—and Pam was hard as nails. But still, it didn't feel right.

Was I to blame for all this? Was it a message, a clue? Surely not? There were too many variables, too much that could, and almost did, go wrong. But what did they care? One more body wouldn't make any difference to them. I dismissed it, at least tried to, but as I sorted myself out, and had a pee as I realized I hadn't gone for hours, there was this nagging, an insistence that this was them testing me. Checking out my new ability to morph over long distances, observing how I reacted, noting the rush to aid friends. Probably so they could update a bloody file somewhere, so when the time came to send someone after me, they'd pick the right guy.

Now utterly depressed, and absolutely knackered, unable to get my fill of food, I figured I'd best get going.

With deep trepidation, I went to find Bernard. I hated riding bloody unicorns, and knew I was in for an ear-bashing.

Such is the life of a poor Necro far from where he needs to be.

Pets!

"Hey, Bernard," I said morosely, as I wandered over to the stables where he was prancing around outside like a right dick.

"Oh, hello," he said glumly. "Come to demean me and treat me like a cheap bike, have you?"

"Yes, that's exactly what I've come to do," I snapped. "Sorry, been a long, hard night. I hurt, I'm hungry, and I have to fulfill my note. Look, I'm sorry, okay, but Phage thought it was for the best. Can we do this, please? I promise once we get back to the others you can go home. I just need my bike."

"It's okay, I don't mind. I'll stay."

"You will?" I asked, surprised.

"Sure. We're a team," he said brightly.

"What are you up to?" I asked suspiciously.

"Me? Nothing. Just helping out. You look after me, after Betty and little Kayin, so it's the least I can do."

"Oh, thanks. I appreciate that." Bernard had never been like this. He was always uppity in a special kind of way—he was a magical unicorn and I wasn't. He did everything under sufferance; it was just his way. Maybe fatherhood had changed him. "It has been a long time since we rode together, just you and me. Years and years."

"It has. Shall we go?"

"Yeah, I guess." Bernard was unnerving me. Why was he being so kind?

"You don't look well, Soph. You look tired and sad."

"I am both of those things, and so much more, old friend. Anyway, we gotta do what we gotta do, right?"

"Yes, but we're allowed to moan about it as we do it."

"Haha, I like that." I adjusted the stirrups and tied my pack on tight, then remembered the gun so nipped back inside and left it for Pam. I used the spare key she'd told me about to lock up, then left her to her beauty sleep. She'd feel rough in the morning, but at least she was alive.

I struggled into the saddle, almost said, "Giddy up," but stifled the urge with a boyish giggle, and asked nicely, "Can you take me to Tyr and Woofer, please?"

Bernard whinnied, then trotted out of the courtyard with some fancy moves so the horses could admire his perfect, sleek white coat and awesome, sparkly horn.

I hated to ruin the moment, but as we passed the stalls I whispered, "Bernard, it's the other way."

"Oh, right." Bernard hung his head and moved fast past the staring horses. Poor guy, he was trying.

We left Pam's and had to navigate lanes and main roads, but it was the middle of the night, the world was as black as my fractured soul, and Bernard was in a funny mood, so we made amazing progress. He wasted zero time in getting up to speed, and before I knew it we were flying up the motorway faster than any vehicle had ever gone. Behind us we left trailers of sparkling joy. A rainbow of wonder as Bernard dismissed the rules our world lived by and dashed through the air powered by pure, unadulterated magic.

I held on for dear life, even though it wasn't strictly necessary. But moving faster than a supersonic jet has that effect even after so many years and so many unenjoyable trips. I was cocooned in Bernard's power, a bubble of safety. The world tasted of strawberry bon-bons. The air was sickly sweet with the scent of roses, and my usually dark mind was crowded with images of puppies rolling around in fields full of poppies while I laughed and hollered like a right numpty, a stupid grin on my face. Such was the power of a unicorn, a being as timeless as the world itself. Born of pure magic and destined to live forever. Or as close to it as you can get. Entropy still held Bernard in its merciless clutches, everything came to pass eventually, but for all intents and purposes, Bernard would live on and on, and one day might even be smart. Although, I didn't think there was enough time in the universe for that to happen.

And then we arrived. In less than an hour, we had traversed the distance. Most of that was him gaining speed or slowing down to take sharp turns, only destroying three hedges, two gates, and one massive bloody road sign. Must have been some kind of record.

Arse numb, superficial wounds beginning to heal after Phage's gentle whispering, but still fresh enough to allow me some good moaning, and with visions of puppies clearing, I jumped down and said my thanks. Bernard wandered off to take his fill of grass, a poor meal, but he could go home as soon as he had recovered. Phage was in for a right earful.

I stared down at my two most faithful companions. Tyr was curled up between Woofer's legs, tight to his tummy. Both of them snored like old men; neither awoke to defend camp from an intruder. Bloody poor show, but they needed their sleep.

Envious, I curled up beside Woofer, draped an arm over his side, and was lost to dreams in seconds.

The morning brought lots of excited hellos, the youngsters insisting on me recounting every detail of recent events, and then me having to endure a blow-by-blow account of their evening of freedom. It mostly involved sleeping.

Bernard was gone. What was with him? He was acting out-of-character. Hadn't moaned as much, done less stupid stuff, and he would never leave without saying goodbye.

I called Phage to check in—she was fine. Bernard was back, and she agreed he was acting odd. She thought he was down because Jen was paying him less attention. Bernard loved her with all his heart, but as Kayin grew along with Jen, so the pair had begun their bonding. We'd have to ensure Bernard didn't get left out. Kayin was as large as her parents already. She was stronger, certainly smarter, and a right willful handful. Maybe the old guy was just tired; kids were knackering.

Next I called Pam—she was alive, so that was good. The doc was about to arrive so I left her to it, making her promise to call me or Phage if she needed any help with anything.

Then it was just me and the guys. We ate breakfast, I sorted out my gear, and then it was time to go. Again.

"Let's get this thing done," I told them.

"Tyr will guard the sky," he said proudly.

"Woofer will guard Soph and sniff out bad men." He wagged his tail, ready for praise.

"And I will ride like the wind. Let's go!"

Woofer barked, Tyr roared, I walked over to my...

"Where the fuck is my bike?" I asked my motley crew of utterly incompetent twatheads.

They exchanged glances, then looked about the trees. Tyr flew around, Woofer sniffed all over, then they returned and both said, "It's gone." Woofer sat and looked at me expectantly, Tyr likewise, as though the news deserved a treat.

"You guys are killing me here. Are you seriously telling me that while I was off saving a damsel in distress, you two just slept the whole time and let some opportunist passerby steal my bike from right under your noses? You're a bloody talking dog imbued with magic from all those who have nurtured you since you were saved from certain death," I lectured. "And you're a bloody fire-breathing, acid-vomiting, immortal dragon. You can't even guard a bicycle? You're a disgrace to yourselves and I'm embarrassed to know you."

They hung their heads in shame.

I was so annoyed I didn't even bang on about it. What now?

"Guess we're walking the rest of the way. No way can I morph. I won't be fit enough to fight. Come on, and if either one of you dares to make an excuse for your utter incompetence, I will ban treats for a whole month. Understood?"

They understood alright. I stormed off in a huff. Bloody stupid animals. I should have come alone. It would have been less annoying and a lot quieter.

Trudging North

The advantage of cycling as opposed to walking, apart from speed, is that there is less chance to talk. Walking meant Woofer could wax lyrical about the beauty of rolling upside down, boast about how great he was at jumping, how fast he could run, his ability to count to one, and how amazing he was at chasing after balls. My bottom-heavy mutt spent fifteen torturous minutes explaining to me how great he was at sleeping by the fire, with a blow-by-blow, realtime recounting of his every move to get settled and the fact he thought of absolutely nothing while he did it. I was just glad I'd left the gun at Pam's, because it would have been either him or me.

He recounted at least fifty times the tale of when he found a whole pack of sausages in the garden and how tasty they were. It didn't matter that I repeatedly told him we were having a barbecue, and he didn't find them, he nicked them, and everyone but him went hungry, because he had selective hearing when it suited him. And it suited him just fine when the topic was thievery of sausages.

I even called Phage to tell her about my woes, and got zero sympathy, but the moment I hung up, Woofer began blabbering away about the different balls he'd played with over the years. I was enthralled!

It wasn't even just the constant monologue. Riding meant you got some wind in your hair, some air up your shirt, not just the suffocating heat pounding at your head.

And if I was asked once to play ball, I was asked a hundred times. I didn't have a ball, and he knew that, but he was a positive kind of guy so that didn't deter him in the least.

My luck worsened when he did actually find an old tennis ball.

"Soph play ball with Woofer?"

"I already told you, I don't have a... Oh."

"Throw ball for Woofer? Soph loves to throw balls. Watch Woofer fetch?"

"Fine," I sighed, needing an excuse for a break anyway. I was knackered, and we had a very long way to go. The road was beyond hot—we had to use the verge because the asphalt was literally melting here where they'd obviously used an inferior grade.

We clambered over a rotting gate and into a field. There weren't many trees, but there was a single large oak in the middle of the otherwise empty field, so we headed that way. Once in the shade, I shucked off my pack, tried to unstick my shirt from my back, then just took it off and hung it up to dry.

I threw the ball for Woofer and he ran hell-for-leather after it then returned it before I'd had chance to even take a drink.

Woofer mumbled something but it was garbled. I could read the thought, but I was acting dumb, just like my buddy here.

"What's that? I can't hear you. There's a ball in your mouth."

Woofer dropped the ball and said, "Soph throw ball again for Woofer?"

"Yes, fine." I reached for the ball. Woofer grabbed for it and looked up at me, hope in his dopey eyes.

"How many times? I can't throw it if you pick it up. Why do you always do that?"

Woofer dropped it. "Soph throw ball for Woofer now?"

"Yes, okay." I reached for it. Woofer grabbed it and pranced about making a grunting noise. "Idiot dog," I moaned.

I moved to my pack, so Woofer ran in front of me and dropped the ball. "Throw ball now?"

"Last chance." I bent for the ball and...

I ignored the fool and rested against the tree then took a long pull on the water bottle. The field was barren, what was that about? No animals, no crops, no nothing. There were a lot fewer animals now though. The supposed methane problem had finally been addressed and with a vengeance. Across the globe the rearing of animals, particularly beef, had declined in a major way. More land was given over to vegetable production, but that wasn't without issues. Many argued there wasn't enough fertile land for such an endeavor, others said that was a lie. We had to stop eating meat and eat only what we grew instead. Others countered that animal meat, particularly chicken and other poultry, was more efficient. And besides, how would you fertilize the land without animals? Was everyone going to start composting their poo? No, they wouldn't. I didn't have solutions; I just knew I loved a steak.

So much of what we were told was opposed by others, making it impossible to know what was right, what was just an agenda.

Who was I to know the answers? I didn't even know what electricity was and I'd been around before it was even a thing. Was it invented? Could you invent electricity?

Drones buzzed across the field. Necrodrones. Watching me. Taunting me. Since the advent of drone technology, I'd often wondered if the whole sudden jump, going from no electric to TVs, computers, smart phones, drones, tiny cameras, satellites in their thousands, and the whole digital age, wasn't tied to the Necroverse.

Was it all sped up? Did the jump happen so our lives could be televised for an audience somewhere? Were there millions of people watching me lean against this tree, exasperated by my dog? Did strange, wobbly green beings with eyes on tentacles sit in front of huge monitors with multiple feeds, each one streaming live the events of a poor, half-dead Necro in a different part of the world? It was fanciful, but lately I'd grown increasingly aware of the drones and the fact they could well be screening my every move to more than just a single person monitoring me. I recalled an old movie. The Truman Show. Was that what this was?

Was I nothing but a game show to another race? Or was there a secret society, a select few, for whom this was their entertainment? But what about before? Technology was a truly recent worldwide phenomena. How would they have watched before that? Maybe they hadn't. Maybe it had all been part of a long-term plan, leading up to this.

I laughed, and shook my head at such fanciful ideas. Stupid. But still, it nagged at me.

"Fine, I'll do it," came a dour voice from behind the tree.

I jumped up, startled, then relaxed as I realized it was Bernard the Wonder Twat. "What are you doing here? Thought you moped off back home?"

"I knew you needed me, so I came back," he said, about as sullen as a unicorn could be.

"You don't seem very happy about it. You didn't have to come. But thanks. I think I might need you. I'm beat."

"So am I. No speeding this time," he said. "We take it slow."

"Sure. Um, how'd you hear about the missing bike? I assume that's why you came?"

"Phage told me. Came and found me. Lucky for her she can't understand me. I wasn't best happy. Couldn't you just buy another one?"

"Um, yeah, I guess I could. But not here. There aren't any bike shops."

"Oh, that's how it works, is it?"

I took a moment to process that. "Yes, you have to go to a shop that sells bikes to buy a new one. You alright, Bernard? You don't seem yourself."

"Well, now that you ask." Bernard proceeded to tell me how hard it was raising a young one, that he wasn't getting enough sleep, that there were too many demands on his time, that he didn't get enough attention from Betty, and nobody appreciated all the hard work he did.

When he'd finished, I asked, "So, you wanted any kind of an excuse to get away and have a break? Am I right?"

"Absolutely not!" he said, indignant.

"Come on, this is me."

"Maybe a little."

"So why'd you go back in the first place? You should have stayed. Using all that energy."

He said something but I didn't catch it. "What was that?"

"She said I had to look after Kayin," he mumbled.

"Ha! I knew it! You're under the hoof."

"Am not. I'm my own unicorn. I've lived almost for ever. I do what I want, go where I please. I remember when you humans were just grunting and bashing each other over the head with clubs. I do what I want."

"As long as you aren't back late and you do the babysitting. Trust me, I've been there, done that, got the hessian overshirt to prove it. Don't fight it, enjoy it. Believe it or not, these are the best days of your life. You've never had kids before, right?"

"Never. Now I know why."

"You love it really."

Bernard gave a big cheesy grin and whinnied as he shook his pure white mane.

"Play ball with Woofer?"

I looked at my ever-hopeful friend, eyes lit up with anticipation, tail sweeping back and forth across the dusty earth.

"Sure, Woofer. Now, let go."

Woofer ran off with the ball still in his mouth. I smiled. What more could a man ask out of life?

As if reading my thoughts, Tyr raced across the open field, showing off, and plummeted when he spied a rabbit. In one fell swoop he caught the creature with his claws and dispatched it. He then tossed it high into the air and roasted it with an impressive stream of fire, then caught it again as it fell. He glided over to us with it in his mouth.

"Tyr is mighty hunter now." He tore at the meat hungrily.

"You sure are. Seems like only yesterday you couldn't catch a bug. Now look at you." It was a fine display. He had come on in leaps and bounds. Still daft as a brush, but that would change too. For one still so young, Tyr was showing all the signs of being an exceedingly dangerous creature once fully matured. Hell, I wouldn't want to be on his bad side now.

I was going to ask him if he wanted to share his kill, but when I looked at the utter mess he'd made of the poor rabbit I decided to leave him be.

Sparked out because of lack of sleep, too much fighting, and basic stress overload, I missed what Tyr said at first.

"Sorry, say again."

"You are sad your friend is hurt."

"Yes, I am. I don't know why she was targeted. It doesn't make any sense. Pam's a good person."

"She has killed others?"

"Yes, but only because of the notes. That doesn't make her bad."

"No? Isn't it bad to kill people? You tell Tyr that is wrong."

Woofer was listening, Bernard too. I was in a pickle here. "It is wrong to kill, but the notes are different. Or if somebody is trying to kill you, then if you have no choice you have to kill them."

"So if it is okay to kill because of the note, then the person trying to kill Pam was not bad."

"Yeah, kinda. It's not black and white like that. There's no choice."

"Everyone could stop obeying," suggested Tyr. "No more killing."

"Then we'd be killed."

"By who?"

"I don't know. Whoever does the notes. If you don't obey, you get eliminated. Sometimes whole families. Mass refusal has been tried before. The number of Necros dropped perilously close to zero. So we do as we're told. But it doesn't mean everyone's bad. Pam isn't bad."

"Pam kills. Killing is wrong. Pam is bad." Tyr munched on the charred bones as he watched me closely. Woofer and Bernard wouldn't take their eyes off me either.

"Look, none of you should kill. And Tyr, you especially must be careful. You will be very dangerous when older. Yes, even more dangerous than now, so you must never kill unless absolutely necessary."

"To survive?" asked Woofer, probably the first time he'd been this serious in his life.

"Yes, to survive. It's twisted, these notes, it makes us do things we don't want to do. But if we refuse, we die. So I guess it's down to that. Would you rather die, or kill someone? Many choose to die. I get it, I really do. But I made my choice, and yes, so did Pam. I still think she's a good person though."

I shifted my gaze away from them. There was no easy answer to any of this. But Tyr was right. None of us were good people. We made our choices.

Reluctantly, I told everyone it was time to go. As usual, the days were getting away from me. Something always happened. I couldn't recall the last time I simply rode somewhere, killed a dude, and got home without there being any stress—apart from the killing, of course.

Travel Blues

The road was busy, far too crowded for my liking, and the checkpoints were rammed. It took an age to get through them, and it seemed the police manning the points had endured thorough re-training. Gone was the quick glance at the papers and a bored wave through the cordon. Now they were checking everything closely and asking a lot of questions. Even with my special pass, it was a major inconvenience.

Violence was brewing.

I wanted no part in it. More and more people were being turned away for having insufficient reason to be traveling. They were told in no uncertain terms that they had to go home. Unless it was for work or unavoidable family issues, with proof, then they weren't allowed to continue. People were angry. The lockdown had gone on too long. Years and years now, with only brief respites for folks to get the travel bug out of their system.

I understood the frustration. Although it had become the norm to stay close to home, people still wanted to break free and do as they wished. This was not a police state. We had hard-won freedom to defend, and we'd had enough. There were also more cars. New fuels were available on the black market for reasonable prices thanks to enterprising farmers, so people didn't have to wait years to use their meagre quotas any longer. Sure, there was a risk of massive fines, even imprisonment, but nobody got a long sentence for having bootleg petrol. Meaning, for many there was little to lose apart from a stern telling off and being made to turn around. But there were plenty of stories of people being locked up for a few days, so it was never worth the risk for someone in my position where time was of the essence.

"What's the hold up this time?" I asked a fellow rider as we trotted along beside each other at an excruciatingly slow pace.

"They're going through everyone's belongings," he told me, his face dark from the sun.

"Bloody hell, this is ridiculous."

"Tell me about it. It's taken me hours to get twenty miles and I have a long way to go yet. Hey," he looked at me, suddenly suspicious, "you aren't undercover, are you? Not a nark?"

"Haha, no, absolutely not."

"Cause you have to say if you are."

"Um, I don't think I do, but I'm not. Damn, I don't have time for this."

"Where you going? You got important business, have you? That's all the reason you can have if you want to get through."

"Yeah, I have something going on in Liverpool."

"I'm heading further north. Got a thing too," he chuckled, then winked at me. "This shit is getting fucking old. I bet you remember using cars too, right? Not like the youngsters who think this is normal. Can't go anywhere, can't do anything. Everything takes bloody ages using a horse, and when you do get home there's no bloody power for a cuppa. Can't watch the TV, and the missus is going spare because there's no juice for the washing machine half the time. Damn, never thought I'd miss the dishwasher so much. Now I have to wash up. I fucking hate tea-towels. Bastard things. This crap is killing me."

"I hear that. Things have tightened up a lot these last few years. It's a different world for the kids now. At least they aren't playing as many computer games."

"Ha, tell that to my three. They sneak off and use all the power quota. I took the consoles away, but my life isn't worth living now so I'm gonna cave and give 'em back. Bloody bastard government. They gotta get this sorted."

"They will. Give it time. Things will be back to normal soon enough. At least, there will be a new normal."

"I'm not holding my breath," he grunted.

The queue moved forward so we finally got close to the checkpoint. My new friend shielded his eyes then groaned.

"Christ, will you look at that! These new police think they own the bloody road. Acting all high and mighty, pushing people around. Look at them."

I craned to the side to look around the small group ahead of us; the police were just politely asking for people's papers and then going over them and their belongings carefully. Nothing violent, or even rude, but it was damn slow and ridiculously thorough.

"They're just doing their job. Think about it," I told him. "How many jobs are there now that let you be outside for part of the day? Everyone else is working at home. Stuck inside, having to account for every watt. We have more police than in our history because it appeals. It's that, or be a farmer. And we know how tough they have it. The rules for them change every bloody day."

"Yeah, yeah, I know all that," he said gruffly. He removed his wide-brimmed hat and rubbed at his sweaty face. He was red and pissed off, I got it, but it wouldn't achieve anything. "But I just wanna watch the TV and have a cold beer. Not get home after all this stupid slow traveling and have to feed the bloody horse, argue with the wife, drink a warm beer if we can even afford any, and stare at a dead screen because the kids have used all the power. I can't even get a hot shower half the time. And my bloody deodorant and shampoo are bloody bars, like soap. What the fuck is that all about? I want to roll my deodorant on, not rub my armpits like a fucking backward caveman. They'll have us grunting and forgetting how to read next. It's fucking evil."

"It's because there's no plastic. It's progress." I did miss toothpaste in a tube though. Using tablets felt weird, and I remembered a time when all you did was eat an apple and wait for the inevitable rot.

"Screw that. I want steak, and wine from France. Not this shit they make here. And I want to arrive in comfort. I want to be allowed to go where I want and not answer to these bastards."

"Get a unicorn," I told him, smiling.

He glared at me, face reddening. "You being funny?"

"Just lightening the mood," I told him. "See you." A gap opened as someone was pulled aside then taken behind the cordon for more checks, so I moved ahead in my line and left him a few paces back. He was trouble; I could smell it on him. So much for the lack of booze. He reeked. Some homemade concoction, no doubt, but judging by the booze sweat, he was pretty much constantly drinking. Sun and booze did not mix, not that I wouldn't mind a few cold beers myself. And he was right about the wine. With no imports, we had to drink British, and we had a long way to go before we got it right.

I reminded myself how lucky we were at home. The Necropub, solar and wind arrays that still worked to a degree, and being careful with our power meant our life was comfortable. Maybe I should get some big old mill wheels and make the animals run around to generate more power? Bernard would love that.

"What you got to smile about?" asked the man as he came up beside me again. "You laughing at me?"

"Huh? I'm just a happy kinda guy. No, I wasn't even thinking about you. Cool it, okay?"

"Don't fucking tell me to cool it! I'm fed up with this crap. I want to sit in my car. I've got a bloody Lexus. I want to relax in it with the air con on and listen to Coldplay."

I shuddered. "Okay, sure thing."

"What, you got a problem with Coldplay? Don't like a Lexus?"

"No, no problem. Whatever floats your boat."

"Next," came a call from ahead. The line had cleared; it was our turn.

I put on my best face, the one without the grimace, and Bernard dutifully moved forward. "Don't forget to keep your head up high," I reminded him. "They can't see the horn but they will sure be able to feel it if you poke their eyes out."

Bernard's head rose and he walked carefully. He was an old hand at this, but I never trusted him to remember.

"Papers please," asked the policeman perfunctorily.

"Sure thing, officer." I smiled at him, and handed over the papers I had in my hand, ready.

He checked them over, noted my information on a small tablet, then asked me where I was headed.

"Liverpool. I have business there."

"And what business is that?" He gave me a hard stare; a test to see if I'd squirm.

"I'm afraid I can't say, officer. I would like to, but I'm not allowed. It does say on my papers. Sorry about this. I understand it's not normal, but I honestly am not allowed to tell."

"That's fine," he said with a grin. "Just checking. You'd be surprised how many forgeries there are, how many people try it on. Usually they cave when I give them a good glare, haha. Well, everything seems in order. I just need to check your bag if that's okay?"

"Sure, no problem at all." I smiled back at him; he seemed like a nice guy. Just sticking to the rules, doing his job.

"Hey, how come he gets special treatment?" shouted my new friend from his exhausted horse. "What, he a posh twat is he?"

"No need for that, sir," said the policeman dealing with him. "Everyone is being checked. There's no need to raise your voice. Now, your papers please." The frustrated young man held out his hand for the papers, but the pissed guy didn't even have them ready! I mean, c'mon.

"Wait, they're here somewhere. Hold on." He fumbled about in his pack and eventually handed over a crumpled mess of information to the waiting officer. The one about to check my gear was watching closely, so were several others. They knew a troublemaker when they saw one.

"Can I go?" I asked.

"One moment, sir, be with you soon. Don't worry, this won't take long." The officer moved to my pack and began to open it up whilst keeping an eye on the guy causing the hold up.

I missed what he was told, but judging by the way his face nearly burst, it was so red and angry, I knew it wasn't anything he wanted to hear.

"I will not turn around, you bastard. I have every right to go there. I have business. What, it's one rule for that smug bastard and another for us regular guys? Is that it? No, I know my rights. I demand you let me through."

"Sorry, sir, and please watch your language. You are not permitted to travel just to make a purchase. You must stay in your own zone unless it is an exception. You have no papers for that. You must return home."

"But I need those bloody horses. I told you, I have the money. I can pay."

"That's not the point, sir. There are strict travel restrictions for a reason. We must conserve energy. Everything costs. Travel to buy things is not permitted. Order it online, that's my recommendation." The officer made the mistake of smiling at him, much as I'm sure he'd have preferred to punch his face in.

"Online! Are you a fucking moron? I can't buy it online, can I? It's a fucking horse. Two horses. Do you know how hard it is to get a horse at the moment? I need to go pick them up. Now let me through." He dug his heels into his knackered horse's flanks and snapped the reins. Spooked, the horse whinnied and darted forward.

"Stop!"

"I'll get him," shouted the guy dealing with me. He sprinted after the horse as it knocked several officers aside then came up short at the barrier across the road.

By now, over a dozen officers had surrounded the man and ordered him to get down. He shook his head, arms waving wildly, and shouted, "I need to buy those animals. Let me through. I know my rights."

"Dismount this minute," an officer shouted.

"Freeze," shouted another, as the man reached into his pack.

"You fuckers!" He pulled out a pistol and waved it around. "Move, all of you. Move, or I'll shoot."

A shot rang out. For a moment, he was still, a look of shock on his sunburned, angry face. A hole in his forehead oozed blood; he slid sideways off the horse and face-planted into the road with a crunch.

People all around me screamed. Horses scattered, furthering the confusion and panic. Travelers ran in all directions, others tripped over each other, everyone worried they'd be next.

Bernard remained stoic, probably contemplating his navel or wondering if he had one (did he?). Woofer whined but stayed still. I just sat on my "horse" and waited it out.

A veritable cloud of drones buzzed overhead, no doubt having recorded everything from every conceivable angle. It was a good kill; there would be no comeback on the officer who pulled the trigger.

They got the man out of the way, bundled him into a waiting ambulance, which I guess meant they expected this now and then, then moved his horse to the side of the road where an officer tended to it.

My guy came back over and said, "Sorry about that. It's happening more and more. Hey, you didn't run like the others. Damn, you're cool. You should sign up."

"Yeah, maybe I will," I said, nodding.

"Let's get you through, shall we? No need to check your bags today." He saluted and I saluted back. Bernard moved forward without being told, Woofer jogged alongside, obedient mainly because he was scared.

We rode maybe a quarter mile until we were out of sight of the checkpoint, then I asked Bernard to move to the verge. We had the road to ourselves, nobody behind us yet.

I jumped down and patted Bernard's flank.

"Well done, both of you. That was pretty hairy. You did great. Woofer, you were so cool. You were frosty." I patted his head then crouched down and held up my hand. We high-fived.

"Woofer not scared. Woofer very brave."

"You sure were. Good job. Now listen, both of you. That was exactly how to deal with situations like that. You always stay calm, act extra polite. Never give anyone a reason to give you grief. They don't want the hassle, and we sure don't. Be courteous and it gets you a long way. And when trouble kicks off, be the cool one, the one they leave alone. Don't panic, don't run around freaking out, never give anyone cause to go after you. It's how you survive."

"Woofer wanted to bite angry man."

"Yeah, me too. But that would have been bad, wouldn't it? Got us into trouble. Right, I think that's enough of this road. Let's get a quiet route so we can relax and avoid the checkpoints. They only bother with the main roads. It's too much hassle for everyone to go the long way around, everyone's in a rush, but I think we'll actually make better time if we add ten miles or so to the trip. No risk of getting shot either." I checked the various options on my phone then mounted up again.

We stuck to the motorway for another mile, then took a left turn onto a nice quiet stretch where all we could see were fields and more fields. A lot were covered in solar panels, many more were bare, just skeletons of framework waiting for the installation. The stripped field of a mere hour ago made more sense now. How much land would they cover in panels? Would there be enough left for food production? I had to assume those in charge knew what they were doing. But it was hard to take such things on trust.

We plodded along, getting shade from the high, unmanaged hedges, but the air was thick and slow, no breeze, and very uncomfortable.

"Wait, stop here," I told Bernard, suddenly overcome with an urge I couldn't quite articulate.

Bernard pulled up at a narrow gap in the hedge. Nothing but a slit where the maple and oak refused to grow. It was dark and impossible to see through. I jumped down and crept forward cautiously, unsure why, and feeling rather foolish because I had only ever been attacked by a hedge once and it was my own fault. As I advanced in full ninja style, apart from the shining white unicorn and whining dog, something nagged at the back of my mind. The knowledge was there, just tantalizingly out of grasp. What was this place? I pushed on through and entered the edge of a dense forest, hidden from the sunken road by the towering hedges. It was cool, quiet, and inviting.

I popped back out onto the lane and beckoned them in. "Come on, it's lovely. I think we'll go this way for a while."

"Is it quicker?" asked Bernard. "I'm worn out."

"Um, I think so. Not sure. But it's almost chilly in here. You like it fresh, don't you? I bet there's a lovely cool stream somewhere. Imagine that."

I didn't have to tell him twice. Bernard shoved through the narrow gap and Woofer followed along dutifully.

We found ourselves in a slice of English paradise.

Cool and Dreamy

Tyr had been quiet since before the checkpoint. I worried for a moment that we'd lost the little guy, so ducked back out of the forest and called for him mentally. He replied faintly, but within a few seconds I spied him closing in fast.

With a languid beating of his wings, he drifted down and alighted on the top of the hedge.

"Where you been?" I asked. Sunlight caught the orange sclera, glinting like malicious emeralds. Sometimes his eyes scared me.

"Tyr watched from high. Practicing seeing far. Very good eyesight now. Saw angry man raise gun. Dead now."

"Yes, very dead. He was stupid, should have known not to get angry. Sometimes you have to control your anger, Tyr. Let it wash over you. When people are shouting and acting wild, that's the best time to remain calm. It allows you to think clearly, consider your next move. Often it's the edge you need to emerge victorious."

"Tyr is calm."

"Yes, but you're like me. When the bloodlust is upon us we can't hear anything. We lose control, let the violence take over. Only do that when you know you have to fight and there's no choice. But bide your time, my friend. Remember, until you have to fight, stay calm. Let the violence out only when you know you can give yourself to it fully. Understand?"

"Tyr understands." He bowed his long neck but kept eye contact. Sometimes, I found it hard to believe he was a real dragon. Maybe because he was still relatively small, maybe because it was so fantastical. Probably because I'd raised him from something no bigger than a newt. Like your children, you always have that image of them being born in your mind, no matter how fast they grow. Would I still see that when he was larger than a car? Big as a bus? Would he really grow into such a fearsome creature?

"Come on, I found this awesome shady woods."

"Tyr likes the sun. The heat. I will follow above the trees."

"Suit yourself. But I'm off to cool down."

He took to the wing and I returned to the gloom to join the others.

An hour later, I had no idea where I was and didn't care. There was zero signal on my phone, no way to choose the correct path, of which there were many, and Tyr was lost to my calls. I caught glimpses of the sun, so knew we were still heading roughly north, but beyond that I had no way of knowing if we were ten steps from a road or in the middle of nowhere.

Every time we came to a junction of the narrow tracks, I simply intuited which turn to take. I just knew. It was a puzzle, a real concern, as I hated things like this. All "wave your arms in the air and go wibbly wobbly" because there was magic afoot. Although, there most definitely was. This was akin to the witches' paths. Invite only, no outsiders. Impossible to navigate, the paths took you to your destination whether you liked it or not. Hocus Pocus bullshit.

We were on just such a journey and it didn't sit well with me. I should know what was happening. It was there, tantalizingly out of reach in my mind. The knowledge of this place. Memories, or something like that. Either I had been told, or I had been here. But when? And why? And for how long?

Had some batty old crone done a number on me and made me forget? Had I pushed it away on purpose, or was there simply no room in my head for this particular set of memories?

I was clueless.

On the other hand, it was freaking awesome. Cool, dark, and quiet. Soft, spongy moss underfoot. Tiny flowers peeked through the undergrowth, saplings and ancient gnarled oaks and endless majestic beech trees co-existed happily—I half expected an Ent to walk by and offer us a lift.

But none came. More's the pity.

After several hours, it was obvious I should have been concerned. I wasn't. I was having a lovely time. Bernard and Woofer were quiet, my mind was all dreamy, and nobody had tried to kill me.

There were things to be done though. I had to get to Liverpool. How much time did I have? How long had I been away? I should know this, but I couldn't hold on to such thoughts in this place. What was worse, although it didn't feel worse, was that I plain didn't care. When was the last time I had such peace? No jangling nerves, no deadlines, no bubbling anger hardly suppressed, no unexpected daemons in my kitchen? No problems at all?

It was a problem.

I stopped suddenly, aware enough to know there should be a problem. There was always a problem. I was on a job. I should be stressed and questioning myself, cursing the Necronotes, those behind it, and going over and over yet again what the point was and who the bastards were.

The lack of such weighty issues crowding my mind was cause for concern. Why was I so chilled? Clearly, it was this forest. This magical, mysterious forest. Maybe we could all come and live here? Yes, that would be awesome. We could hide away. Nobody would find us here, not even the drones which were entirely absent. Was it off-limits to them too? I was kidding myself; that was wishful thinking. There were spies everywhere. No, we couldn't hide out. What about school? What about the zoo? What about the Necropub and the Brewer? What about the short dude in the basement? What was his name?

I laughed, mainly because I was freaked out.

"Play ball with Woofer?" asked my best buddy hopefully, but I could tell his heart wasn't in it.

"I think you lost it," I told him dreamily.

"Woofer just run after Soph. Play chase?"

"Maybe later. You feeling okay there?" I asked him.

"Sleepy."

"Yeah, me too. Bernard, how you doing? Your mind okay?"

"You saying I'm dim?" he asked, glaring.

"Guess you're fine. No weird goings-on in that awesome head of yours? Not feeling a bit strange? Anything seem odd to you?"

"You mean the magical forest? No. Seems normal."

"But you just said it was a magical forest! That doesn't strike you as odd?"

"I'm a unicorn." He shrugged, like that was answer enough. Guess it was.

"Let's have a rest. I'm beat. I bet we're near the end now. There aren't any forests this big around here."

"There's one," said Bernard.

"Where?"

"Wow, you really do need a rest," he told me.

I relaxed my entire body without giving such an act a second's thought, then slid to the ground and spread my arms wide, smiling at the cool moss, the lovely shade, the beautiful black eye in the sky...

Wait.

What?

The "eye" as I called it, wasn't an actual eye, that would just be nuts. It was a savage rend in the fabric of our world, which made much more sense. An elongated, ragged slit maybe twenty feet long and seven wide, hovering above the trees, looking like it was about to swallow me up whole.

Maybe it was.

The emptiness inside shimmered and wobbled like jelly made from night, with some sprinkles added, but I got the distinct impression someone was watching, maybe about to do something. What, I couldn't even imagine. I just hoped I wasn't about to be sucked up then dumped into an active volcano. Tyr would love that, me not so much.

As the light of day was vanquished due to its descent, I peered as deep inside as I could. A brief glimpse of a dim room—at least my mind told me it was, even with no walls I could see—that gradually grew brighter yet without any warmth or cheer. Cold, heartless, a place devoid of joy. My heart juddered. Through the murk, I saw thousands upon thousands of small sheets of paper flapping like a flock of demented seagulls, swirling in a tornado, reaching higher and higher, never ending. The noise was as deafening as a cave full of bats as they slammed into each other then careened off, caught in a vortex that carried them ever upward.

Light caught the bleached paper, glinting off the corners. A twisted kaleidoscope of pale, refracted weirdness bounced out and brought the whole scene into stark clarity for a moment. Each sheet appeared to be attacking another, but it was just the manic movement that made me think of it like that.

Archaic, fanciful calligraphy pens darted this way and that like missiles, scrawling jerky, ink-splattered words on the paper, writing names on the folded pieces, and up they flew, snapping and almost tearing each other to shreds.

The clarity was gone, the scene faded to black, the eye winked out of existence without warning or even an impressive *pop*, and I was left gasping on the ground.

Was that real? It felt real, but it also felt like a dream.

"Did you guys see that?" I asked, as I jumped to attention. Already the power of the forest was calming my nerves, fogging my mind.

Woofer was asleep and snoring, Bernard had his horn stuck in a rabbit hole. I freed him by calling him names and prodding his rear, then said no more about it. I settled down next to Woofer and soon joined him in sleepy land. Just a few minutes, I told myself. It was so nice here.

I dreamed of giant eyes in the sky. They were Tyr's. Cold, and full of malice. Purple and orange that snapped to unblinking dark slits.

Through the Woods

I awoke with a harsh craving to smoke. I packed old faithful with a good wedge of tobacco, lit her up, and puffed away to get it going. The nicotine hit beautifully, strong and harsh, so I sat there for a while, enjoying the moment, slowly coming back to myself from a dream-state.

Had I seen the eye? What did it mean if I had? Who would show such a thing? I truly wasn't sure if it was real or not. This whole place had my head cloudy, as though I was being sucked into the gentle slumber of the forest and might never escape.

"It's time to go," I told the others.

They were slow, clumsier than usual, and not very communicative, which was a clear sign this place was messing with us. We trudged onward while I smoked obsessively, following tiny trails then wide paths, leading us somewhere, but where?

"Come back when the time is right. Until then live your life. Forget about me." I could picture the old man saying those words to me as he shuffled about in his hobbit house, a memory as clear as day yet entirely lost until now.

Where had that come from? It was real, I knew it, and with it a whole host of other memories flooded in.

It was a long, long time ago when I was a different person entirely. I was young, angry as all hell, and utterly reckless. The world owed me, and I intended to make it pay. My life had been awful. I'd got out as soon as I dared, knowing what awaited me. For many years, I ranted and raved against the injustice of it all, before finally accepting I was a pawn in a game I could never hope to understand let alone win. Now that was a feeling I could still get behind!

A wizard lived here then. Maybe he still did. If I was in this secret sanctuary, then it meant the pass I'd earned by my actions all those years ago, when I finally turned from being a boy to a man, was still active. Could he still be here after so long? What had he said all that time ago? And how had I forgotten about him entirely until now? I hadn't given it another thought since I'd left; that wasn't right at all. My past haunted me, all the loves, the children, the lives lost, the deeds done, and this was one of the most important of my formative years. There was no way I could have forgotten.

But I had.

An old man, ancient even back then. Archetypal wizard. He used a gnarly staff, had long, lank hair, big beard, eyebrows with a life of their own, and turned me on to smoking a pipe. There was a weird house full of books, strange objects, and enough herbs to satisfy any witch, where he spent his time deep in study, or lifting ethereal rocks he ought not to peek under, but that was his thing. He was truly archaic, had knowledge and understanding of things no other I had met knew even now, and he took me in, was kind, when I somehow ended up in his company without ever understanding why.

Why now, after so long? I'd been this way before, many times, never got caught up in this place. As we continued, so snippets of my past punctured the shroud of dreams. I recalled getting lost, then feeling a presence. A guide. I followed, aware I was being manipulated, but at ease with it, understanding it was for my own good. I'd met the man, Mawr, and he'd invited me inside, fed me, told me tales, helped me understand who I was, what I was, and told me I should never give up. To keep going and one day we would meet again.

"Guess today is the day, old man."

"Soph is talking to himself," said Woofer.

"And Woofer always talks in the third person."

"Woofer want to know what third person is."

"Bernard want to know too."

"Bernard, did you actually just make a joke? Haha, good one."

"Um, no," said Bernard.

"Oh well, keep trying. So, in case you don't know, which you don't, although you might, Bernard, an old—"

"Wizard lives here," said Bernard. "You met when you were young, he calmed you down, and helped you become a man. The usual lost young traveler story, saved by a magical man in the woods."

"How do you know?"

"I'm a unicorn. There's a lot you don't know about me."

"I think there probably is," I told him. Not for the first time, I wondered if he could read my thoughts. If he answers this, I know he can, I told myself. I turned my head sharply to catch Bernard off-guard but he had his horn in another rabbit hole and I knew I was just being silly. I did a double take just to be sure, but he was still stuck.

At least some things never changed.

Smoking like a chimney, and I wondered if this was Mawr's influence as we got closer, we sped up and soon found ourselves on a nice wide path through the most ancient heart of this woodland. Birds sang, foxes and other secretive creatures moved freely through the woods, I swear I saw a bear, there were boar and deer and other things I never caught more than a glimpse of. I sensed their thoughts, happy and content in their own private sanctuary. Nice place to be alive.

After a short stroll, aches and pains fading, calm settled on our merry group and we enjoyed the chance to just be in the moment. No weird stuff, no phone calls, nobody trying to kill us. Bernard didn't get stuck, Woofer stopped bugging me about playing ball, and all was well in the world. Living somewhere like this sure was tempting.

And then, just as I was about as calm as I'd ever been, we exited the canopy and found ourselves in a small clearing. A large log store sat nestled amongst the weeds to one side, an outdoor kitchen beside it. A well-tended, obsessively geometric vegetable patch took up most of the cleared land, at odds with the small, overgrown orchard and long grass elsewhere. It was all rather untidy, in a controlled way. Set almost hidden in a hillock was a small hobbit house. Low, carved front door, curved windows, green roof with a chimney. Smoke rose languidly, as lazy as the air.

Birds darted to-and-fro, a horse munched on hay beside a small stable block, and chickens pecked at the dirt. They all ignored us, like we were here every day.

Memories slammed into me like a wrecking ball.

Fresh to the Necroverse in all its foulness, I'd made only a few kills and was disgusted with such acts, yet understood enough about myself to know I would do what was necessary to survive. It made me sick to my stomach and I railed against the world for the things I was made to do. Angry with my parents for forcing a cruel childhood upon me, where I was stuck in a foul school that impressed upon us the future that lay before us children. We'd been encouraged to unlock what gifts we had and practice them incessantly.

They trained children to become killers, and I will never forgive my parents for making my formative years so miserable. As soon as I was old enough, I left the school, left my family, and made my own way in the world. It was hard, it was brutal, and I barely scraped into adulthood. But I made it. I got my first note, then my second, then found myself here. An old man called Mawr let me act out my frustrations, and I stayed for a while. How long, I couldn't recall, but it must have been weeks. He taught me things, he eased my mind, and I became a man whilst under his tutelage.

Snippets of my stay flicked past in brief spurts of information overload. Of him showing me ways to release my anger when right, of how to calm myself when it wasn't appropriate to show emotions, of how to heal myself, how to hunt, and how to communicate better with the animals. Mostly, he taught me that people could be kind and caring and not judge.

So why now? Why was I here?

A man exited the house and closed the door behind him. He walked slowly over, about as typical a wizard as you could imagine. He was just as I remembered. He still had his gnarly staff, the hair and beard had grown wilder yet was still silver, the dancing eyebrows able to startle a ferret at a hundred yards remained draped over intense blue eyes, and he wore a wizard's cloak. He was also smoking a pipe.

I smiled.

"Soph, you have arrived," he said, puffing a cloud of blue poison.

"Seems that way," I said, then I grinned as I ran forward and hugged him. He smelt of tobacco and wood smoke, of the earth and fresh leaves. It was like hugging the forest. Mawr gripped me tight with strong muscles; we stayed that way for some time. I felt like I'd come home. We released eventually, and stood back to get a look at each other.

"You're exactly the same," I told him.

"And you have aged, I see. It suits you."

"Figured I'd better look like a grown-up. I guess I finally am one."

"And a fine man you have become. And who are your fellow travelers?"

"This is Woofer. Woofer, this is Mawr, an old friend."

"Woofer like Mawr. Play ball?" he asked hopefully.

"Haha, that sounds like fun. Maybe later, Woofer?"

"And this is Bernard," I told him.

"Hello," said Bernard.

"My, a unicorn. You are very welcome, Bernard. All of you. And there is somebody else, I understand?" Mawr looked to the sky as a silhouette closed in on us.

"Oh yes, he's a handful, so watch out. Damn, this is weird. Why am I here?"

"Haha, yes, rather strange. Don't worry, we can talk later. For now, let's enjoy the day."

Tyr came down fast, circled us, shot up, took a hard dive, then glided across the clearing before sweeping up to land on Bernard's back.

"Tyr is here," he announced, chest high, eyes gleaming.

"Stop showing off," I told him.

"And get off my back, you overgrown lizard," said Bernard, as he turned and nudged Tyr with his horn.

Tyr flapped down to the ground then walked over to stand beside me.

"Tyr, this is Mawr. He is to be treated with respect, as though he is family. Mawr, meet Tyr. He's a wyrmling, only eleven, but he's growing fast and can breathe fire now."

"Tyr is Tyrant of the Sky. I can make acid and hunt my food and I'm best friends with Jen and when we're older we will be together all the time."

"Jen's my daughter," I told Mawr.

"Yes, I know."

"Huh? What? How?"

"Because I am a wizard, Soph, and some of us can see these things. Plus, there's this thing called the internet. It helps. Haha."

"I guess. But how could you find me on the internet?"

"Your name. There aren't many people called Soph. But before that, for hundreds of years, I watched you, just as your masters have spied on you. Although, they have always had other means at their disposal."

"What? I'm not following. And should we be talking about this? You know the rules. Do you still get notes?"

"Everyone gets notes while they are able. And I am more than able. But rest assured, there are no spies here. No cameras or microphones, no drones, or anything of the sort. No way for another, no matter their abilities, to see what happens here. Don't forget, I am old, and I am powerful, even if I do say so myself. Nobody comes here, or sees here, unless I say so. It is the way I retain my privacy. There is much you do not know, but now is the time for some answers, yes? If you want them. For there is no denying that once you learn these things, there is no going back."

"I guess you already know I'm torn about that, then?" He nodded. "So, how come I forgot all about you? I know for a fact I owe you a lot, even my life, so to forget, well, you did a number on me, right?"

"Yes, as you call it, I did a number on you. Haha. You had much still to learn, and things to do, and it was not right for you to return. But now you have. So let us celebrate. A drink, perhaps?"

"I could murder a cuppa," I told him.

"Tea it is then. And let me see what I have for you," he told the others.

I felt instantly at ease, as though the intervening years had been a matter of days. But it had been over three hundred years. Such a huge volume of time seemed impossible, even though I'd lived through it. What must it be like for the truly old such as Mawr?

The old man sorted out the animals with food and water, then we left them while we moved over to his outdoor kitchen and he made tea.

"Here we are, after so many years," he said, eyes twinkling with mirth.

"Yes, it's been a long time. So, you put a spell on me. Whispered to me in my sleep, did you?"

"Haha, yes, something like that. It was for the best. You had to live your life. Such a full life too. Sad sometimes, happy others. It is the way of such things."

"And what about you?" I sipped my tea. It was sweet and delicious.

"I have remained here for the most part. Had a few adventures, always my notes, even had several wives and some more children, but that was long ago. These days, I like the quiet. More an observer than interfering."

"Not at the same time, I hope. The wives?"

"Oh, haha, no. Gosh, no. Just one wife at a time. Fun days. I enjoyed it. Now I rest. I have my work, and I have this place."

"Always something to do, eh?"

"Yes, and I have learned much these last few years."

I smiled at the old man. "By few years, you mean hundreds, don't you?"

"It all blurs together. But yes, hundreds. You have done well, Soph, lived a good life. But things are different now."

"You say that like you know. How?"

"I am a wizard. We know. I may not be the best, but I am good, and that is not to boast. It is merely fact. Things can be seen if you have my abilities. The witches know this, but many choose to focus on other pursuits. They do love their exploring. But I watch our world closely, events that affect other Necros. And you. I always watch you. You're like one of my sons. I care for you."

"And I care for you. I can't believe you made me forget. What else have I forgotten?"

"You have forgotten much, you have learned much. That's just the way of these things. But you do want some answers. I see that. And yet, you know that you cannot."

"We're talking about the notes, just to be clear?" He nodded. "Then no, I don't want to know. I can't. But things have happened, weird stuff, even by our standards. "

"Yes, you have been marked. It happens to some of the best. You are being tested."

"Tested? By who? And why? And I'm just a guy, nothing special."

"Oh, but you are. You, your family. You are special."

"What does this all mean? You're being cryptic, you wily old bugger. You going to tell me straight what this is all about, or not?"

"Soph, you may not know it or have accepted it, but your name is known to those like me. Those who study the Necroverse, the matters of humankind at least. You have shown remarkable prowess. You have limited gifts but use them well, and are a rare specimen. This is only the beginning."

"I'm just a dude who won't bloody die," I mumbled.

"Indeed. As I say, rare. You will never get the answers you seek, the truth about the notes, as that would be impossible. But you have already learned some things, and been shown others. I see this, I know this. You understand I have the gifts of a sorcerer? That I can read the future, picture the past, foretell events?"

"I know. So you can see my future?"

"Not like reading a book, no. But I see the potential. I see the knowledge you have locked inside. All learned by seeing you, by following you, by settling my mind and letting the future of the young man who came here play out in all it's variations. There weren't as many options as you would think."

"That doesn't mean you know my future, not for sure."

"No, of course not. But I know you, therefore I can envision what might be. I don't pretend to understand all about the notes, and what I have learned won't really help you, but know this. You are a rare man, you are known, and they want you to understand this. Maybe that is why you have been given glimpses, although I suspect there are other reasons I cannot comprehend."

"Do you know where the notes originate? I saw something, in the woods. A vision. A swirling vortex of notes, millions of them, with the names being written."

"Interesting." Mawr leaned close. "This is where they come from. I have caught glimpses, but never as much as you. Do I know who does this, and how? No. Do I want to know? Yes. But I will never know. Nobody will. Some things are beyond us all. Too complex, too dangerous. But you have seen more?" His focus was intense.

"Yes. I saw how they dispose of the bodies. A portal, a hole opening, taking them away."

"It is how it is done. My, haha, you really are progressing at an astonishing rate."

"And who does it? Is it elves?"

He leaned even closer. "Why elves? Why do you ask?"

"I fought one, four years ago. He let slip, or maybe wanted to tell me, something about his masters, about them watching. It was vague, and he was a right smarmy git."

"They are like that. Understand, Soph, that many races, even some humans, watch the necroverse unfold in many ways. Some watch the slaying, it entertains them, others watch the banal, the everyday. Those with rare gifts have this ability. They can follow a person's life, see the notes and the battles, and they adore it. They have their champions, can follow you through your life like a TV show. They can tune in, watch the past, guess at the future. Maybe this is what your elf referred to?"

"Maybe, I'm not sure. So, let me get this straight. Some races and some humans get off watching us slaughter each other. But they aren't the originators?"

"The notes endure. They are the Necroverse."

"But only for us humans. Why? It isn't fair."

"Such is our lot. Some believe the notes have made Necros a true force to be reckoned with. That through our yearly ordeal we have become something other than what would otherwise have been possible. That it is necessary.

That this will lead us somewhere. Others believe we are just plain unlucky. A cosmic joke if you will. Aliens having fun at our expense. Another race as yet uncovered. So many theories."

"And you? What do you believe, old friend?"

"Oh, I don't merely believe. I know." He winked at me and drained the dregs of his tea.

"You know?"

"Yes. It's God."

"Oh, haha, you had me there."

"Haha, I did, didn't I? Seriously, understand this, Soph, it will help you with your life. We do not know. Nobody knows. We can watch others, we can intervene, we can screw things up or downright refuse, and there are Necros who do not participate, but be assured, nobody knows the true provenance of the notes. It is not our place. Nobody has ever known. Some think they have the answers, but are always proven to be wrong. Some things just are."

"Thanks. I think. So why am I getting these visions? These snippets?"

"Maybe someone is playing with you. Maybe the notes themselves have decided to offer you this knowledge, to allow you to relax, to understand a little more. Maybe it is an accident, but I doubt that. I have seen it before. The older you become, the more you experience, the more the Necroverse opens to you. You have unlocked something. Leveled up, isn't that what they say? You have taken the next step. Allowed a glimpse through the veil. But you will never know the truth. Never have all the answers. Do not seek them out. They will see, and you will be eliminated."

"That helps, I think. Damn, these fucking notes."

"Still the same foul mouth, I see."

"Yeah, sorry."

"Just be careful. Do not be tempted to cross the line. It will lead to your destruction."

"I don't plan on it. I can't help but wonder, but I know how this works. But hell, why say anything to me? Did you ever try to find the answers?"

"Not directly. I have studied the history, followed many paths to garner knowledge, but even though they cannot watch me here, they see me when I am away from home, so no, I have never pursued the final knowledge. Think of them like the Constables, like me. Able to read the slightest tic, a small mannerism, the way you move, speak, any and all of it. It allows those with the ability to read the future, see many outcomes. They are all of that and much more. If you break the rules, they know, and then you are gone. Tread carefully, my friend. Tread very carefully."

"I intend to."

"Now, tell me of your past. The happy times. You have a daughter and a wife? What else?"

While we had another cuppa, I told Mawr of my family. Happy stories that made me long to return home. It was a good life; I needed to be back there with them. Mawr told tall tales of his recent wives and the joy of being a father again, and it was a pleasant few hours.

I had a lot to think on, but when I tried, I realized he hadn't actually told me much beyond, "Don't be so fucking nosy, you'll get killed. I don't know, nobody does. Deal with it."

Maybe that was all the advice I needed.

"Don't suppose you know much about dragons do you?" I asked, partly to change the subject, mostly because Tyr was a bloody handful.

"I know some. You are lucky to have such a creature. I always wanted one, but I don't have the room."

"Yeah, he's going to get pretty big. At least, I think he will. So, what can you tell me?"

"Come with me."

Mawr rinsed out the mugs then we headed to the house. I called for Tyr and Woofer to join us. Bernard sulked, but he'd have to wait outside.

How to Train Your Dragon

Inside was exactly as I remembered. Cluttered, cosy, warm, and dusty. Mawr wasn't big on housework—he actually swept dust under the old rug by the fire until it got too lumpy. He had a lifetime's worth of collectibles in his compact home. Think wizard mind. Jumbled, very full, lots of knowledge, loads of random crap, a terrifying amount of power, and you'd have it just about right. He had books galore, a ton of strange objects, many of which were magical, and a serious fetish for *chibi* plushies, which I totally did not pursue.

"Ah, here we go." Mawr dropped a weighty tome on the table. Dust billowed up, making me sneeze. "It's a bit out-of-date, but it's mostly accurate. Haven't seen anything to better it yet. He waggled insane eyebrows—must be an old wizard thing, they love a bit of eyebrow-waggling.

Tyr peered down at the book from his position on the table, then scowled at Mawr.

"Mawr kill dragon to make the book?"

"What? No, of course not, little wyrmling. This was made long before my time. Written by my ancestors. Granted, things were different then. We had much less understanding, but yes, it's bound with dragon skin. Nobody killed one, mind you. It's from an unfortunate creature that perished. Another story, another time." He waved it away with a gnarled hand, then opened the book.

"Wow!"

"Indeed. Full of just about every kind of dragon there has ever been. With names, family trees, skills, strengths, weaknesses. There are diagrams of biology, best as they could figure out, and plenty of entries about how dragons grow, what to feed them, and how to treat them. Although you might want to skip that part, it's definitely not how we do things now. Oh, here's the section you want." Mawr flicked past beautiful image after beautiful image, the painting so lifelike the creatures seemed ready to jump off the page, and stopped at a chapter rather clunkily titled How Dragons Grow and What to Expect.

"Well, I'll leave you to it. Plenty to do. Wood to chop, supper to make. You will stay for supper?"

I was about to say no, but then thought better of it. I had days left, so there was no need to be rude. "We'd love to. Thanks."

Tyr and I began to read. Okay, I read it out to him. He was a dragon and couldn't, and never would be able to, read the human language. A dragon's brain simply isn't wired that way, that much I did know.

"Look at this. It says you can expect to live for many thousands of years and grow to be, bloody hell, as big as a bus. Not that it says bus, but that's the size."

"What's a bus?"

"Big. Bigger than lots of houses."

"Tyr want to be like the big bus."

"Yeah, I bet. Okay, that won't be for a long, long time, when you are very old. Even older than me."

"Gosh." Tyr's eyes went wide; hard to imagine for such a youngster.

"Ah, here we are, all about your development from a young age. Says to hatch you need periods of cold, then extended heat. Well, I got that bit right. Accidentally." I tickled Tyr under his chin. He moved into it; little guy loved a chin scratch.

"What else?"

"So, you are meant to grow slowly, never force it. A dragon should be kept locked up until... I think we'll move on. This was written a long time ago. When ten or so, depending on the development, you should be introduced to the flesh of humans. Hell, they really went for it."

"Tyr had flesh at seven. Became mighty."

"That was my fault. Anyway, it says about ten. Then you should be allowed to develop naturally for the next ten years. No more human flesh and blood. Too much can make you change at the wrong rate. Although it says if you cope okay then it can be introduced earlier. You take on the gifts of those you feed on. We know that part. You must be handled every day or as often as possible by those who wish to control you. Bloody good luck with that," I muttered.

"Tyr behaves," he said, puffing out his chest.

"Sometimes. Once in your twenties, you will suddenly put on a rapid growth spurt, going from roughly the size of a large dog, maybe even sheep size, to doubling almost every year for a while, then it will slow, and then you will just gradually get bigger over many years. Centuries actually. Meaning," I told him, "by the time Jen is of age, twenty-one, you will be big, but not large enough for her to ride you. That might be a few years after, or maybe more. Guess we'll just have to wait and see."

"Tyr can't wait!" he hopped about on the table, excited to be able to fly with Jen. I couldn't even imagine such a thing. I didn't want to.

"No, me neither. Okay, what else?" I flicked through several pages back and forth, and looked up feeding, the acid thing, and fire production. There were numerous entries about them never drinking, but blood didn't count, the acid was a byproduct of fire, which I'd learned the hard way, and then there was a chapter about a dragon's abilities.

"Here we go," I told him, close to his limit of concentration. "After your first feed on the blood of a Necro, preferably human, but doesn't have to be, your abilities will rapidly increase. You can communicate with all creatures, same as many Necros, you can always understand your master or mistress, even if they can't communicate with other creatures, and you will be able to become basically invisible once you reach a certain size."

"How big? How big? Tyr can become ninja dragon."

"Christ, I can only imagine. Well, you're pretty good at it already. Sometimes I can't see you. But it says probably after your second kill you can simply vanish, poof, whenever you don't want to be seen. You can also camouflage, as that takes less energy, but if you need to, you can blend perfectly with any surroundings. Tyr?"

He was asleep on the table.

I continued to read. There was a lot about the different kinds of dragons, although it was mostly markings and body-type. The pertinent information was the same for them all. There was even a chapter on dragon poo, which I absolutely skipped, but damn, these guys were thorough. What interested me was how his mind would develop as he aged. Seemed dragons were pretty much on a par with humans up until adulthood, but unlike us they continued to change over centuries. For a good few hundred years, Tyr would be companionable and often obedient to those he grew up with, but once fully mature, between five-hundred and a thousand years, he would slowly become aloof, less interested in humans, no matter the bond, and would slowly drift apart. Until one day, far into the future, he would isolate from everyone, crave solitude and peace above all else. He would hide in places we were unable to follow, sleep away centuries at a time, even thousands of years, only coming out when he got a calling. What that calling might be it didn't say. It was unknown, but there were stories of dragons emerging after the slumber of millennia, wreaking havoc, then retreating, never to be seen again.

Eventually, they would disappear forever. Off to unknowable, unreachable realms, where they would live for an eternity. Doing what, nobody knew.

The main takeaway was that although Tyr may have begun his change a little early, he was fine as long as he didn't make a habit of feeding on humans. I just had to keep him in check, let him develop slowly like Jen, learn as he went, obey the rules, and at some point, maybe a few years down the line, he could feed on another person. Then he'd grow very fast, be invisible, and a right bloody handful unless I was super-strict. I'd make sure that happened well before Jen was of age; she'd have enough to deal with apart from having a dragon going haywire.

I rubbed at my eyes then closed the book. Dust kicked up; motes danced around the gloomy interior. The fire crackled. It was stifling in here, so I left the animals to their dreams and went outside for some fresh air and to find Mawr, see if he needed any help.

Somehow, I woke up beside a crackling fire outside the gnarly wizard's house.

"What the...?"

"Ah, you're awake. Sorry about that, bit of an oopsie." Mawr grinned sheepishly.

"What happened? Ugh, my head feels fuzzy. You been playing tricks on me, old man?" I asked gruffly. I hated all this wizard crap. Wands and staffs and bloody dusty tomes next to skulls. Never was my thing.

"Sorry, I put the kibosh on a fella a few centuries ago and now it's just a habit to leave a ward up when I'm out and about. Runs itself, and it's usually just me here. What's a poor old man to do?"

"Give a warning to guests?"

"Haha, you always were very funny. Wild, but funny. Did you learn what you needed to know?" Mawr poked the fire with a stick, just because you have to, don't you? Law of fire or something. If it's lit, mess with it.

"I think so. Basically, he's gonna be a handful. He needs Necro blood now and then to keep the fire burning and to fulfill his potential, and will go from being daft as my unicorn to being as grumpy as me."

"That's dragons for you. Be warned, Necrosoph, dragons are unruly creatures. Very dangerous. They have a mind of their own. They are not like pets. They are smarter than us. Know things we never can, and you must keep him close or he will forget all about you, or think nothing of destroying you. They are loyal until their last breath, but only if you keep that bond tight. They must be family, or they will be your enemy."

"Yeah, I know." I scratched my head. "I'm kind of wishing I had never started this. Okay, I love the little guy, but I have to think of my daughter."

"He is a boon for any Necro. She will do well with such a companion. Just ensure he knows who's boss. She must assert her power over him regularly."

"I'll insist on it. So, what's for supper?"

"All in good time. First, a gift."

"Whoa there! Oh no you don't. This isn't some damn quest where I level up every time I meet someone from the past, no matter what you say. Come on, gnarly old man in the woods giving me the power of what? Invisibility? Magic doors? A wand? I don't want a wand. I don't do magic. I do Soph. Hard as fuck and no messing about. That's me."

"As I always knew it would be. You hated the spells, the whispers, the wands and crystals even when a lad. No, it is nothing like that. Although," his eyes twinkled, "I do have a nice wand if you're interested?"

"No thanks. I've got enough on my plate as it is."

"Very well. Then what would you like? Just out of interest. Before I offer you my gift."

"Can't say I've ever thought about it."

"Liar," he laughed. He could see right through me.

"Can you help me to read minds? See the past and the future?"

"I can do those things. Do you want me to?" He leaned forward, studied me intently.

"No. Haha. You nearly got me there, old man. I don't want those gifts."

"Then take this instead. Here." Mawr handed over a large matchbox, the old-fashioned kind that contained long matches for lighting stoves like we had at home.

"I'm good for matches, but thanks." I took it as he kept his hand out, bouncing his wizard eyebrows like this was their last chance to party.

"You are a zoolinguist, you can talk to the animals. A special gift, although not as rare as some. Inside is your salvation. Care for her. Be gentle, treat her well, and let her sleep. She will help when help is needed. She is from the old times. Very rare, almost extinct. Be kind to her. I know you will."

"Can I look?" I asked, unsure what to expect, and no idea what he was talking about. He nodded. I slid back the outer case carefully.

Inside was a tiny dormouse, cute as cute can be. She was curled up, her tail over her face, snoring away. I don't think I'd ever seen a creature as content in all my life. She snuffled as the matchbox shook in my hand, then curled up tighter and continued her hibernation, if that's what she was doing.

"Only wake her when you need the assistance. She will sleep through anything. You can stomp on her, squash her, bash her, toss her in the air, and she will not awaken. But if you call her name sweetly, ask for her help, it shall be given."

"But I wouldn't hurt her, do any of those things."

"Soph, my dear young lad, you are a man of war. You *will* squash her, throw her, drop her, splat her. Let us be truthful in these things."

"So how can I stop that?"

"It won't matter. The box is protected. It is unbreakable, can only be opened by you, or those you entrust, so our little sleeper is as safe as if she were inside the deepest hole in the ground. Nothing will hurt her, wake her, or interfere with her in any way. Let her sleep, call only when needed. Remember."

"I will. And thank you. What is her name? How should I wake her?"

"Her name is Malka. She is a faery."

"You nearly had me there. No fae. No way. Here." I handed the box back but Mawr refused to reach out for it. He just stared at me, long and hard. And kept on staring.

"Awkward," I said, nervously.

"Keep her. She is yours."

"Fae are trouble. At least, that's what I hear. A rare thing like this? It's asking for grief. I've got enough worry already. No fae. Ugh, what were you thinking?"

"I was thinking that you have just started down a road that is more arduous than you could ever imagine. That you will be lucky if you survive long enough to even begin your quest. That you need your companions, your wife, your daughter, and any other help you can find. And that includes Malka."

"What bloody quest? I'm not on any quest."

"Aren't you?" Again with the wiggling eyebrows.

"No. I'm not. Here, take it. Her. How'd you get her anyway? What's she doing being a dormouse? Bit weird, isn't it?"

"Is it? Is it though?" Mawr prodded the fire; sparks danced high into the night sky. He was gone.

"Bloody wizards," I moaned. I peeked into the box at Malka. She was snoring happily. What would I want with a sleeping mouse? What would I want with a faery? And I wasn't on a quest, was I?

I followed the old man inside. My stomach rumbled as I opened the door to a wall of heat and intense smells. At least I'd die with a full stomach. I recalled his cooking from my youth. I was stuffed for days afterwards. Looked like a penguin waddling about.

Woofer got his first, Tyr was allowed to sit in the open fire and eat a slab of roasting venison, which I wasn't happy about as it taught him bad habits, and Mawr and I tucked into the most delicious stew I'd had in over three hundred years. It was like no time had passed at all, when truth be told we were strangers. So different, yet somehow so alike.

Definitely Back at It

After a restless night on rough blankets, and insufferable wizard snoring, I was ready to go by break of dawn. Itching to go, literally. Mawr shook my hand with his iron grip, patted me on the back, and told me to drop by again in a few hundred years. I promised I would if I could.

"Look after Malka. Remember, only call her when you really need her help. She can be grumpy."

I waved behind me as we went on our merry way. Mawr's cryptic cackle echoed through the trees then was cut off abruptly as we were enveloped by the ancient woodland. I turned. The clearing was gone. Nothing but a path so hard to follow it might as well have not been there at all.

We traveled for a few hours through the intense solitude of the ancient land, then just like that we were out. Bernard almost fell out of the woods, so forceful was the ejection. The path was gone, the woods closed to visitors.

Bright, clear skies greeted us with intense heat. Drones buzzed angrily overhead in huge numbers, a crowd of people swarmed the road, shouting and screaming, police vans with sirens blaring blocked the way, and someone was mumbling something unintelligible through a loudspeaker.

I preferred the woods.

What's a weary, irritable Necro to do when confronted by such a scene whilst riding a unicorn, a dragon on said unicorn's rear, a freaked out Lab trotting alongside, and a dormouse faery in his backpack?

After Tyr had flown off, I told Bernard to ride on into the melee and kick anyone who got in our way. Yeah, I was in that kind of mood.

The sirens were almost deafening, so loud I couldn't hear what the press of people were shouting about. Nevertheless, they moved aside as Bernard weaved cautiously through the throng. They closed the gap behind us, but a path opened ahead like they knew we were coming. That's the power of a crowd.

Woofer was utterly freaked, so I called him to jump up. He made it halfway up my leg then I hauled him onto my lap and he sat there, happy as you like, lording it over the mess of humanity below. Tyr hovered well away from the drones, almost invisible.

At the front of the crowd of angry travelers, nearly all on foot, a few on horseback like myself, and scores of bicycles, I had no choice but to stop. The way was blocked by dozens of vans, cars, and well over a hundred time-worn police. Gone were the days of the bobby on the beat with a truncheon and a smile. These lot were in full battle gear. Helmets, visors, vests, leg protection, and wielding MP5s.

We were so close too. I could see the river from here. Liverpool was only a stone's throw away. How had the woods spat us out so close to our destination? Mawr was a sneaky old bugger.

"What's going on?" I shouted to another dude on horseback beside me.

"No idea. Nobody will say. I just want to get home." He did a double-take at Bernard and Woofer then added, "Nice horse. Want to sell it?"

"How much?" Bernard whinnied noisily and shook his head, perfect mane slapping at my face. "Just joking," I laughed. "Or am I?" I whispered.

"I heard that," said Bernard.

"No you didn't."

"What was that?" asked the man.

"Nothing, just talking to the, er, horse." He gave me a funny look. Screw him.

The crowd shouted to be let through the cordon, but the police were having none of it. The loudspeaker droned on, but it was gibberish. People pushed from behind; they were getting crushed. Bernard was antsy, and I was in culture shock after the woods. The crowd surged, unable to stop those behind. We were pressed forward against the line of police with hard shields to stop anyone passing.

Around me, people listed their complaints to the officers, like they could do something about it.

"I've got no electricity."

"I had to travel to get food I could afford."

"Why can't we have batteries? It's a bloody conspiracy!" This one got a massive cheer from everyone.

Scenes like these had become more and more common as the new order tightened its grip. More were hungry, water supplies had become intermittent in places, electric was a luxury now, and there was only so much people were willing to put up with to save our planet. Never mind other countries were in complete meltdown with zero electricity, no fuel to run sewage treatment plants, or even pump water to their homes. They had no schools, no fossil fuels to burn, and little hope for their populace. We had it easy in comparison, but it was all relative.

"Our house is too hot. The kids are getting ill. We need sunscreen. I didn't get my quota." The brown-haired woman was blistered on her nose, her forearms were dark as the road, yet she had no hat or long sleeves. Go figure.

"Ours is bloody freezing," another replied to the woman.

"Shut up. Liar!" From out of nowhere, she attacked the woman with the luxuriously cold house.

One fight led to another, which led to all-out warfare. Those behind shoved in a panic, until we were all forced forward tight against the police line. They held their ground, pushed back with their shields, told everyone to disperse, but it was beyond that now.

Bernard's horn poked over the heads of the police; I whispered in his ear to ensure he held it high. Last thing I wanted was to kill an innocent policeman. They had families, were just doing their job, and none had been prepared for this. Although they should have seen the signs coming a long time ago.

Bernard did well, remained calm amidst the madness, but it wouldn't last. Woofer was freaked, whimpering and trying to cover his ears. I told him he was a good boy but his tail didn't even wag.

"Okay, Bernard, you need to jump high and fast, but no bloody rainbow dust or anything fancy. Just a regular horse that's scared. Got it? Just high enough to get past the cordon, then we'll talk to the ones in charge and be on our way. Do not make me regret this."

With endless cameras recording every move, drones like flies overhead, and us right at the front, Bernard neighed, although I'm sure he actually said it rather than made the noise, pranced about like a scared horse, then leapt over the shields and landed with grace behind them. Like a show horse, but much more smug.

I patted his flank and bent forward to whisper above the din, "Great job. Nice one. You could win the Olympic showjumping."

"Don't even think about it," he grumbled.

"That's the spirit," I laughed.

I guided Bernard over to the line of vehicles as the crowd went nuts behind us. Armed police crowded around, but not too close. They had horses too so understood their jittery, often erratic behavior.

Before anyone could tell me to get down, or tell me to bugger off back behind the line, I put up a hand and shouted, "Sorry, the horse got scared. And my dog's terrified. The crowd pushed us. We had no choice. I didn't want him kicking anyone in the head. Sorry."

"Nobody's allowed through. We need to sort out numbers," said a gruff guy with a shaved head, a massive beard, and bags under his eyes.

"What's the problem?"

"Tunnels are knackered. Ferries have got problems. Most are out of commission. Can't take the usual numbers. The working one is only running once a day. Fuel shortage. No trains. It's this road, or you can go east. It's open, but they've got more hassle than us. Take your pick."

"Damn."

"Yeah, tell me about it. Road's open but expect it to be slow." He rubbed at his pink scalp then put his helmet back on but kept the visor up. "Look, you can go through, because of the horse and dog, but keep it cool, okay?"

"Sure, no problem."

"Papers?"

I fumbled in my pack, no easy feat with Woofer still in place, then handed them over. He checked them quickly, grunted, then handed them back.

"You're a long way from home. Lucky you've got such a good pass."

"Yeah, lucky me," I sighed, glancing behind.

"Be careful, the city's in meltdown. My beautiful city. Why is everyone ruining it? It won't make things better." He was genuinely sad. Scousers loved their city, and for good reason.

"Everyone's panicked. It's the mass hysteria. One person buys a trolley of toilet paper, everyone does. Then there isn't enough. Now the same goes for everything. You'd think we'd have learned, but no."

"Yeah, but still."

"Ugh, what a mess." Poor guy was beat. Fed up, angry like everyone else, and had to try to control a crowd when he just wanted a quiet life. "Think things will change?" I asked him, genuinely interested.

"They have to. My guess? We'll suddenly find a way to use our cars, have more power, get sunscreen, and things will slowly improve."

"It's working, right?"

"Yeah, better than anyone expected. Slowly cooling, more insects, less methane, but boy would I like a steak. We just have to try and survive until we know the planet can. Okay, gotta go," he said in a rush, as the crowd began to break the cordon. "Hurry along." He turned to the second line of defense and shouted, "Let him pass. Be quick."

I nodded, then Bernard squeezed through the gap they'd created. They moved back into position immediately. I grabbed Woofer as kindly as I could then lowered him a little. Damn, I couldn't just drop him. I moved over to a low wall and eased him down. He dropped to all fours, shook himself out, then said sadly, "Woofer not like crowds."

"Me neither. But I think we're going to have to get used to it, but not for long."

We wasted no time heading down the road with the lucky few who'd managed to escape humanity's communal madness.

Liverpool shone from the other side of the Mersey. An iconic image. St. John's Tower, Royal Liver Building, Port of Liverpool Building, and more. Smoke spiraled high above the city. Liverpool was burning.

Welcome to the home of the Beatles.

We crossed the clean river into madness.

Scouse Madness

The city wasn't in complete meltdown as I'd imagined. I had visions of burned-out cars and every building looted, fires raging, citizens running amok. There was none of that, or very little. As I traversed the city, with its clear air, birds flying everywhere, even colonies of parrots, it was simply joyous.

No cars, that was the key. All our cities, our motorways, our towns, villages, everything was different without the cars. But it was when you came to the large cities that it really hit home. It felt like the end of the world. So empty. So quiet. So clean.

Yes there were sirens, police, ambulance, fire engines, as there certainly were pockets of real problems with gangs on the rampage, downtrodden citizens looting, and all manner of nefarious goings-on, but it wasn't utter meltdown or anything approaching it.

Much of the main shopping zones was just normal. People searching out bargains, spending their hard-earned on small luxuries, but the habits of commerce had changed dramatically. There were endless fresh food outlets now, fewer chain stores—so many had gone bust within weeks of the new regimes—and prices for coffees and sandwiches were low as otherwise nobody would buy. Every penny counted, not that we had pennies now. It was hard to keep track of all the changes.

There were almost no lights on; nobody had a choice in that now. Office blocks were close to deserted. Everyone could work from home as they had a measured quota to allow for the use of laptops, PCs, tablets and what have you.

But life went on. Differently, but not that different. It was cool waving at others on horseback, and Bernard pranced about like a right dick, head held high, loving the attention because he was a damn fine-looking horse.

We weren't here to shop; we weren't here to get looks. We should have been incognito, and here I was on a bloody unicorn.

Drones were everywhere, darting this way and that. Cameras watched everything from buildings. Bikes multiplied like rabbits. People were chatting, others looked like crap and huddled in doorways.

We left the shopping zones, moved to the north-east, into residential areas. Cars remained stationary outside people's homes, either on the roads or in driveways, covered in dust and dirt. The streets were mostly clean. Less packaging, and strict recycling rules saw to that. Plus takeaway was a real luxury.

Street after street, some with grand houses, others tiny terraces, the city had the usual mix. People talked outside front doors, over hedges, in the road, and kids were everywhere. A sight that until recently had been rare for decades. They knew no different, but not so long ago they were all inside. It was deemed too dangerous to play in the streets, and besides, there was too much digital entertainment to distract them. Now they kicked cans, played with balls, ran around being nutters, enjoying the freedom, the outside air.

Parks were dotted throughout the city, thronged with children and adults alike before it got too hot. What day was it? Was it Monday? Shouldn't they be working? Did it matter? I had to check my phone. Yes, it was Monday, July 20th. I had four days left to finish this, and didn't want to cut it too fine. With the crap at Pam's still fresh in my mind, thoughts turned dark as I got into the zone. Put away smiles and friendly greetings, replaced with a hunkering down, my hat low over my eyes. I kept to myself as we moved from an area full of the cries of children laughing and playing, into a darker, less jolly part of the city.

I did a double take as I suddenly found myself in a street empty of people. In mere moments I'd escaped the hustle and bustle to a seemingly dead zone. Houses were boarded up, others had doors missing. No curtains twitching, no people talking, no kids playing. Just emptiness. Abandoned streets. Bugger.

"Woofer, stay close. Do not wander off," I told him.

He put his head down and sniffed the road. "Woofer not like it. Smells bad."

"Just stick close and if anything happens, you run, okay?"

"Never leave Soph. Soph want to play ball?" he asked, hope in his eyes.

"Maybe later, okay? Not now. Let's go around this place. I don't like it." I was getting that chill at the base of my neck. We had to leave. Nothing good here. Nothing nice. I checked my phone quickly, hiding it with my arms, not wanting to show it off. The route took us through here but it was easy to skirt around. We weren't in that much of a hurry. Last thing I wanted was any trouble, and this place had trouble written all over it. Literally. Terraced houses were covered in graffiti. Not the light, fun, cool art kind either. The dark, mean, angry cry of gangs and the forgotten. Of desperate people, of mad people, and cruel, nasty bastards.

Bernard turned, and I didn't have to ask him twice. We headed back the way we'd come, towards a junction. I memorized the route, then pocketed my phone and got Bernard to speed up, but not so fast we couldn't turn at a moment's notice.

The next street wasn't quite as bad, but bad enough. "Let's go faster, Bernard. Get out of here. Just a few streets and there's a park. Anything happens, and I mean anything, I want you to go ahead and wait there. You too, Woofer. If I say go, then you go. You can't get into a fight yet. We have serious work to do later, and I'll need you both then." I wouldn't, but I didn't want to risk them getting hurt. I should have come alone. It was always easier as I had less to stress about.

"Woofer will help."

"No, you do as I say. You too, Bernard. You have Kayin to think of. Kids come first, okay?"

"Okay." Bernard was weirdly quiet, and he didn't even argue. He could sense the tension.

"Then let's go."

Bernard sped up. Nothing crazy, just a good canter down the empty road.

Something tight snapped along my chest and I was dragged off Bernard as he sped onward. A rope was strung across the street, lowered from first floor windows to catch me. As I sailed backwards with the rope now under my armpits, I grabbed it with both hands so I wouldn't smash into the ground.

"Run, both of you. Wait for me where I said," I shouted, as the rope slackened and I dropped to the road. Bernard legged it, Woofer hesitated. Men burst out of front doors. Woofer ran at one and snapped at his leg. A man booted him hard and he rolled away, yelping. Woofer righted himself, shook it off, and went back in for more.

"No! Leave it, Woofer. I order you. Go!" Woofer looked at me, then nodded and chased after Bernard.

Four men grinned at me from the middle of the street. They moved slowly, all cocky, confident they had the better of me. I was easy pickings, had encroached on their territory, and now they would take whatever they wanted. Or so they thought.

"I don't have time for this shit," I mumbled, unfastening my knife so I could grab it quick.

"What was that?" shouted a sly kid with a shaved head and a Stanley knife. He swished it back and forth, sneering.

"Is that meant to be intimidating?" I asked, brushing the dirt off my clothes, but keeping an eye on them all.

He paused, and narrowed his eyes as he studied me. I was meant to be scared; he hadn't encountered the likes of me before. "We'll show you fucking intimidating. This is our patch, our streets, you gotta pay the price."

"If they're your streets, then you're doing a piss-poor job of looking after them. All I see is ruin. You think that's the way to look after a community? Terrify them? Take what little they have? Make it unlivable?"

"Shut the fuck up!" he snarled. With a nod to the others, they ran hard at me.

Knowing how to deal with these situations, I did what any sensible Necro would do. I ran.

With only a vague memory of the layout, I escaped down alleys, darted across streets, but always circling back close to the start. Mainly because I didn't trust Woofer and Bernard to stay put. If they decided to come back, I needed to be able to help them. Bernard could take care of himself if he was so inclined, but he wasn't a murderer. Not on purpose anyway.

Morphing was an option, but a risky, exhausting one, so I just ran, knowing they'd split up eventually. They weren't the smartest, and couldn't even keep up, so it didn't take them long to decide they could cover more ground individually. I circled back around to one of them, and let him hear me. I knew how this played out, so understood one of them would have to die, or at least get a serious kicking, for me to be left to go on my way.

He turned sharply and chased after me, so I ducked into an alley stinking to high heaven. As he ran straight in without even looking, a total amateur move, I pounded a fist into his face, mashing his nose to little more than pulp.

"Fuck." He spat blood and lunged for me. Zero thought or fighting skills. I dodged, and punched him again. His head snapped back but he remained standing. Usually that was enough to send someone running.

"Leave me be, and this is the end of it. You won't get what's mine, but I'll kill you if you continue." I always give a warning to kids like this, it's the way of such things.

"You ain't going nowhere," he said in a strong Scouse accent. "Your gear's ours now. And that stupid dog. Get a bit for that. People are all into their pets these days. Horse is worth a fortune." He cackled through broken teeth; this guy liked to fight.

Rather than keep the conversation going, I did what all good fighters do. While he was blathering on, I charged while he was busy dreaming of his riches. I also played dirty. You win a fight by being the first one to strike and never, ever playing by the rules.

As I smashed him into the brick wall, I clutched his package and squeezed until something popped. He screamed the place down but I just gripped harder. His face turned puce and he batted ineffectively at me as his chances of ever having kids became zero.

From nowhere, he managed to chop me in the neck. My grip loosened and he shucked me off then staggered deeper into the alley as I blocked his exit. He breathed hard and ragged but still wasn't down and out.

A knife appeared, so I drew mine and we squared off.

"You'll pay for that. I'm gonna skin your dog alive while you watch. You hear me? I will peel it and you'll watch me do it." He spat blood again, like it would make me run.

He meant it. I could see the cruelty in his eyes.

The fool rushed me, knife out, so I waited until he was almost upon me, then stepped aside and slashed at his face. He grunted, but turned and came again. This time, I managed to slice his arm, and as I turned to escape his swipe, I grabbed his lank hair and yanked as hard as I could. Skin and greasy locks came away in my hand, leaving a gross raw patch on his scalp.

As he yelled, I smashed the hilt of my knife into his face. His eye split, the lid tore open, and I hammered it again. I was deep into it now, lost to the madness that ensured I wouldn't think about my moves, think about anything, just act on instinct, my reaction much faster than my brain.

He was already done. The fight gone from him.

And yet, from somewhere, he still sneered. "Gonna make it slow," he giggled. Bitter, evil, the worst kind of cruel right to the end.

"You could have walked away," I told him.

Then the animal in me took over once more.

Disobedient Dragons

I grabbed his head tight in my hands and stared into his good eye; the other slid slowly out of his ruined face and hung at his cheek by a frayed optic nerve. Sections of scalp were missing and my fingers slipped on skin and bone, part of his ear was torn off, his teeth were wrecked, his nose broken, but I felt nothing. I didn't even recall inflicting half the injuries.

He knew this was it, and I gave him no last-minute reprieve. Nothing nice, no kind words to send him on his way. I adjusted my grip, then bounced his head back against the wall. Then again, and again, and a third time until his skull cracked and the body went limp. Hair came away in my hands, along with more of his shredded scalp. Brain oozed between my fingers as the corpse slumped to the ground. He left a bloody, meaty skidmark on the weathered brickwork.

"Welcome to fucking Liverpool, Soph" I grunted, as I booted the bastard in the face where he lay, already dead, then turned at the sound of footsteps coming up fast behind me.

I stepped aside from the corpse so the three men would see him. They stopped short of me. Each brandished a knife, one also held a gun. "You killed him! You smashed his fucking head in. You bastard." He raised the gun.

"Listen, he started it, but he picked the wrong guy. I warned him, I told him he could walk away, but he thought he was good. He threatened to torture my dog. Nobody threatens me or mine. Nobody gets my phone, my gear, my animals, anything. Understand? I said do you understand?"

The three men just stared at their dead companion, mute. Then the gun wielder spoke again. "I'm gonna kill you for that. Then we'll have all your stuff, including your oh-so-precious phone. And yeah, we'll slice that mutt up and let it bleed out. He's gonna die slow. Just like you. You're a dead man."

I didn't need this crap, and was knackered from dealing with the dead idiot, although I'd have rather not killed him as it meant complications. But I had to get out of here, sort these fools out first, so I used the hard man act, although it wasn't much of an act. When I got like this I was wild. Dangerous. I knew I had them beat. If it had been me, I would have shot me already, not talked. They didn't have that feral side, a truly violent, willing to utterly let go side that you needed to win every fight you got involved in. I had it. I hated it, but it was me, and I accepted it.

"Look, if you try to shoot me and miss then I will kill all of you like your friend here. Trust me, it's not easy to shoot a person. I killed him because he gave me no choice. I don't want to harm you. But if you try to fuck with me, anything at all, any of you, you die. All of you. Understand?"

"You can't beat three of us," said one of the others. A wiry guy wearing scruffy jeans and a vest. He had nice muscles, and a very cool knife.

"I can, and I will. Look, here we are, chatting, when if you had any sense at all you would have already shot me, jumped me, and stabbed me to death. But you know, you understand it isn't that easy. Because trust me, if you miss, if you screw up in any way, I will destroy you and stomp on your brains. Do you fucking understand me?"

The gun wavered and the man looked to his friends.

"Shoot him. What are you waiting for?" said the muscly kid.

"Do it," said the other.

I knew what was coming. He couldn't lose face, so I suddenly said, "Boo!" and ducked to the right as the gun went off.

The sound was defeating for us all as it reverberated off the alley walls. I ran, still crouching, slammed into the guy with the gun, smashed his hand into the ground, grabbed the weapon as he released it, and was past them in a heartbeat. No morphing needed or considered.

They turned in a panic, and I stood there, hand steady, calm as you like, and told them, "Do not even think about doing anything else. You got off lightly. I'm not in the habit of killing people unless it's for my own survival, so you lot just grab your buddy, get him buried, say nothing to anyone, and get the fuck out of my sight. First, ID. All of you."

Utterly freaked, they handed me their IDs. I took photos with my phone quickly, then handed them back.

"If I hear a word about this anywhere, a mention of my description, anything at all, then I know where you live. If you move, I will find you. You will die," I promised. I pocketed the gun, grabbed my gear, gave them a glare for good measure, then wandered away, whistling, just to freak them out and ensure they got the message.

"Fucking Liverpool," I grumbled again, as I rounded the corner and put my back to the wall to catch my breath.

A few seconds later, two of the men came out of the alley dragging the body with them. They pulled the corpse down the uneven pavement like they were hauling a sack of potatoes. Grunting and sweating, casting nervous glances back at me but not making eye contact. They turned a corner and were gone. What were they going to do with the body? I didn't care, as long as it didn't come back to me.

There were no cameras I could see around here, this was one of endless no-go zones now if you appreciated the government watching over you, so at least I knew I was safe from any unwelcome official questions. There weren't even any drones; guess they got fed up having them shot down.

I sighed, because this wasn't over. This was a surprise, but some people won't, can't, let things lie. They'd had their pride hurt, their manliness questioned, their weaknesses exposed, and the one still in the alley was unable to live with it.

He'd have to die instead.

Minutes passed, my nerves bounced, anticipation building, but the other guy didn't emerge. I knew what was happening, had seen it many times before, and he'd already made a massive mistake. He was building up courage, trying to summon the fortitude, the will, to enter into a fight that very well may mean his death.

There are few people in the world who can enter a fight voluntarily after seeing their friend killed by the man they are contemplating battling to the death. That's not how the human mind works. We are wired for survival. I gave him a choice. Stupid pride was stopping him acting sensibly. His heart would be hammering, he would be sweating, feeling sick to his stomach. Nerves on edge, willing himself to move, to attack, to somehow overwhelm me and emerge the victor. He felt like a coward. He was a loser. He couldn't live with himself after having his manliness questioned. But could he do it? Could he risk his life like this?

Poor guy already had his answer. He waited too long, lost the adrenaline, the murderlust. The unconscious mind taking over and fighting for survival as our ancestors had done when they had no option. But he had an option and it would be his downfall.

I walked away, leaving him to his questions and doubts, because I didn't want to kill him. Why would I? And why risk my own life for no other reason than to satisfy a stranger's sense of personal justice? For this had nothing to do with vengeance for his friend. It was his insecurity.

Tyr called from high above the empty streets. He could smell the blood. I told him to stay clear, that I would call him down soon, but for now he was to remain hidden. He banked off to the left and disappeared behind a large, burned-out tower block. An accusing black finger pointing at the ferocious sun.

Senses still on high-alert, I dodged bags of refuse and navigated stripped-down cars. Many houses had their doors kicked in, tiny dwellings the council had been unable to sell for even a pound coin back before we switched to European dollars and several other currency iterations because nobody knew what the fuck they were doing. It was bleak. A testament to broken dreams, broken promises, and an insight into the madness we lived with now and had for so very long. Mere streets away were large homes with nice hedges and fancy brass knockers, but for numerous reasons, this small district had become home to gangs, dealers, thieves, addicts, drunks, and fire starters. Left to its own devices. Abandoned, just like the people.

"I fucking hate cities," I muttered. A weariness took me over as I walked slowly, watching my footing on the slabs that had become uneven, a breeding ground for enthusiastic pretty weeds with fluffy white heads. Beauty even in the heart of darkness.

"Aargh."

I turned as the idiot ran at me wielding an iron bar, a look of anguish, hatred, and terror on his face. He still had ten feet to cover and had already given away his location and intent. I almost felt sorry for him. I mean, how stupid can you get? Not wanting to draw more attention by using the gun, even though I had time to draw it and fire, I slid across the blackened husk of a Ford Cortina and yanked the door further open as he crashed into it.

Wind knocked out of him, I split his nose, beat down hard on his forearm so the bar hit the ground, kicked the door, which whacked into his chest and sent him sprawling, then raced around, grabbed him by the hair, and dragged the shouting fool into one of a seemingly never-ending number of alleys between the rows of houses. What the fuck was with these alleys? It was like they built the place to encourage crime and fuckery.

He screamed and batted my arms as his hair yanked out, scalp and all. He fell, then grabbed my ankle and tripped me. I came down hard on my backside, right on my coccyx, and lost my grip. He scrambled to his feet as blood poured down his face; his eyes were wild and yet still he didn't run. Apparently decided, he charged me, ready to boot me in the head, but I rolled and righted fast, taking a glancing blow to my thigh. I punched out as hard as I could muster and knocked the air out of him as I made contact with his guts, then followed through with an uppercut. He bounced back, somehow turning, and careened headfirst into the wall. I stepped forward and punched him again. His head spun and he caught his face on a protruding piece of metal embedded in the wall. With a terror-laden scream, he fell back as his cheek ripped free and then, all fight lost, he collapsed.

A sudden beating of wings, a soft whoosh as something flew past my head, then terror in the man's eyes as he somehow focused on what he undoubtedly believed to be hell itself coming right at him.

"Tyr, no! Don't you bloody dare. I absolutely forbid it."

"Tyr hungry. Has to feed. Need blood. To grow. Build fire inside. To burn," he hissed. His tail thrashed and his body shook wildly as he fought inner demons.

"You can't," I told him calmly, although I was panicking inside. "Stay focused, keep a hold of yourself, and do not," I warned, "feed on that man. Stay strong. Listen to me." I was losing him.

"Must feed," he groaned. Tyr's eyes were intense, the orange sclera turning darker, the bloodlust upon him. He battled overwhelming urges as he moved closer to the terrified man who inched backwards until he came up hard against the wall.

"Control yourself. You must," I whispered to the wyrmling. "Fight it, do not feed. You aren't ready yet. You mustn't grow too fast. It's dangerous."

Tyr's strong jaws snapped open and closed as he tried hard to quash the natural urges of such an ancient and wondrous race of creatures.

"Think of Jen," I soothed. I rubbed his flank, careful of the spines that had grown to become hard keratinous shards that could slice you clean open now. "You want to be with her. You love her. She doesn't want this. She's young, eleven like you. You aren't ready. Later, when she's older, when she can cope with you being large and you are of age, then you will feed. Become mighty warrior."

"Tyr does love Jen," he said, eyes dimming, body relaxing.

"That's right, you do. You are a warrior, and warriors know when to battle and when to rest. Rest now, my friend. Take it easy. Breathe deep and let the urges pass you by like clouds on a lovely hot day. Peace. Be at peace." I rubbed his head between long horns that swept back majestically from his skull, past his ears, and partway down his long neck.

Tyr settled. His heartbeat slowed, his body relaxed, and I continued rubbing his head to bring him back to his senses.

The man, forgotten for a lax moment, lunged forward. From somewhere, he suddenly produced a stubby knife and stabbed at Tyr's head. The blade shattered as it hit Tyr's skull, and the dragon's eyes snapped to crimson.

His body tensed, and Tyr simply did what a dragon would do. His head shot forward on thick neck muscles and his jaws clamped down on the man's hand, knife hilt and all. The hand was severed; the man screamed pitifully. Tyr swept his long snout to the side then snapped back, taking a chunk out of the man's face. Half the jaw and cheek were swallowed whole. Tyr, lost to my screams and shouts, my warnings and threats, snapped again. He tore off the entire front of the face. The guy's screams ceased. The wyrmling paused, then chewed on the corpse's neck, hitting the jugular, and drank deeply of the blood still pumping momentarily after death through the guy's sick, twisted veins.

And then it was over. Tyr slumped back, the red faded from his eyes, and he sighed as he turned his attention to me and stared not with affection, but as though I were a second course.

I slapped him hard across his snout.

"If you ever look at me like that again, I will destroy you. Do you understand me? You are to be Jen's. If I cannot rely on you, then you will leave and never return. You will never see her again. Tyr will be alone in the world. We must be able to trust you with our lives. Do you understand me? If I tell you no, you obey. You obey. Do you understand?" I repeated it slowly; he had to believe my words.

"Tyr understand. Tyr sorry. Couldn't help it. He attacked. I couldn't stop."

"I know. I understand. But you looked at me the same way. I am your friend, and your master. Is that clear?"

"Yes."

"Fuck!" I slumped beside the wyrmling. My emotions were all twisted inside. I had never hit an animal, never told Tyr I was his master. We had always been friends. But here was the truth of it. I *was* his master, like his father, and he had to obey my rules. Children had to do as they were told, had to be taught the ways of the world and not have true freedom until they were older. This dragon, this creature more powerful than any other, needed to be guided. If he wouldn't, or couldn't, then as much as it would break my heart, he would have to leave us and never return.

Tyr's stomach rumbled. He belched a geyser of flame, then puked up all over the man's midsection. Clothes and skin dissolved instantly, then the ribcage was exposed and bone dissolved as the acid bit deeper. Again, Tyr vomited, and the man's internal organs popped and spat then he was cut in two as the acid ate through the spinal cord and chewed away at the ground beneath.

I scrambled away and rubbed frantically at my face. I couldn't recall a time when I'd been so concerned about someone I loved deeply with all my heart. The juvenile dragon stiffened, then he began the change once more. The horns lengthened, his body fattened, the tail swished frantically as it almost doubled in size. Tyr's snout stretched, teeth grew, and his whole body shuddered under the immense strain. The ex-wyrmling flickered in and out of view, going through myriad changes all at once. One moment he was red, then green, then blue, then a mangy dog, then a man we'd killed on a hill in North Wales, then this man dissolving before us. And then, unexpectedly, he vanished entirely.

"Tyr, where are you?" I hissed.

I felt his breath at the back of my neck, and for the first time in my life I was afraid of him.

"Tyr is here. Not feel well." I turned and the dragon looked deep into my eyes then collapsed.

"Get up, right now. You haven't finished."

"Tyr sorry," he moaned, clearly not coping at all.

"I know, but we can't leave him like this. He has to go, to vanish. Use the acid, dissolve him completely. Quick, before you can't."

Tyr looked at me, questioning. I nodded.

He dragged himself forward, stood on unsteady legs, then puked all over the guy from top to bottom. He staggered away and collapsed in a foul heap. I watched the acid burn through everything, only stopping when it bit deep into the ground. The man was gone, utterly destroyed, nothing but a steaming, hissing hole in cracked concrete.

I turned to Tyr, shocked at what I found.

Tyr was no longer a wyrmling. He was something else now.

Haunted Memories

"Look what you did to yourself!" I snapped. "You heard what I read from Mawr's book. You know what you're meant to do, how you should grow, and you bloody ruined it!" I was beyond angry, and a little scared. I must never be scared of him; he would know. I pushed it down, let my anger take its place, and I stared hard into Tyr's eyes so he could see exactly who I was, what the deal was here.

"If you ever make me afraid of you again, you are no longer part of this family. Do I make myself clear?"

"Tyr sorry. I love you. I love Jen. Don't hate me. I couldn't stop." His head hung low; his breath came hard and fast.

"I love you too, with all my heart, but family are not afraid of each other. Do you understand? Tell me you do." We held each other's gaze for what felt like an eternity. I saw the understanding grow in those now wise eyes. Tyr read me like Mawr, like a Constable. He saw my fears, my doubts, my concerns. He saw my resolve. That I meant what I said.

"Tyr understands. Understands so much now. Sees so much. I am a monster. If Tyr could cry, he would."

"You are a dragon. A proud, formidable creature. The most powerful creation there has ever been. Greater than dinosaurs." I smiled at him; he loved dinosaurs.

"Tyr is special," he agreed. "But afraid. I could not stop, didn't want to. Forgot about Soph and Jen and family. Wanted food. To burn. To kill."

"And that is your nature too. You're young. You'll learn. Just remember, you are part of a family. You are not alone. No more feeding," I warned. "Look how bloody big you are."

He turned his head and followed the new lines of his body. Even he was shocked. "Tyr large now. It hurts." His body rippled and cracked as the scales slowly aligned.

"It will for a while. You made a big jump, and like the book said, it isn't time yet. So take it easy, no more feeding, and let this new you settle in. You'll find it harder to fly and move for a while, as your spatial awareness is all wrong. It's a bigger leap than before, much bigger, so be careful."

"Tyr will try." He stretched his wings but the alley was too narrow, so he focused for a moment then walked out as he vanished from sight.

I heard the beat of wings and knew he was up in the air, but damn, he had totally disappeared. A short geyser of flame belched from nowhere. I called to him mentally to be careful. Tyr said he was very tired and the man repeated on him. If it wasn't so bloody worrying I would have laughed.

Nursing bruises, knowing I had to tend to the worst cuts, and knackered and sick as the adrenaline dissipated, I went to find the others. We had to rest up for a while. Hopefully, the remaining residents of Liverpool would be a little more welcoming.

Woofer and Bernard were waiting in the park by a tree, trying to look like they belonged. They clearly didn't. Neither of them were city-savvy. I moved slowly, carefully, not sure what damage had been done, but confident it wasn't anything too serious.

"Woofer sorry."

"No, you shouldn't be. You did the right thing, and you did as I asked. Unlike Tyr. Both of you did well. It's a good lesson. If I ask you to do something, then you do it, as it's for your own good. I can't risk losing you guys. Okay?"

They both nodded, clearly uncomfortable with the whole situation. That made three of us. We moved deeper into the park and then settled on a bench in a small garden area where roses scrambled over old walls and nobody would bother us. In the past, there would have been sunbathers and people playing ball, now you just had dog walkers and those risking stretching their legs in the open where the sun held no quarter. The kids had gone home; no playing in this heat. I checked myself over, applied some creams and a few plasters and whatnot, but that was it. I'd live. I was fine. A few lowlifes couldn't take me down.

My bum really hurt though.

I just sat there for a while, painful coccyx be damned, and watched the people coming and going in the main park. I was removed from them and their lives. I didn't belong. Some threw balls for animals too hot to bother chasing, others rode horses, holding umbrellas. Most merely used it as a shortcut from one place to another. Life as usual.

A woman caught my eye. She was slightly overweight with lank auburn hair, and glanced around as though nervous as she walked with purpose through the park. I saw her face for a brief moment. What was it about her? Did I know her? Someone from my past? There were a lot of people over the years; things like this happened on occasion. It had gotten awkward several times when somebody approached me, having to resort to lies and trying to change my accent and pretend I wasn't who they thought I was.

Some believed, others pestered me, were sure I was the man they'd known many years ago, even though they were old and I wasn't. Mostly I convinced them, sometimes not. But what could they do?

In Liverpool though, with all the memories it held, all the people I'd known, the faces I remembered, it was very likely I would recall at least a few folks from a previous life. But this woman, she had something about her.

I decided to follow her.

It was stupid, it was reckless, it was absolutely not the right thing to do for so many reasons. But I knew I had to.

I mounted Bernard, then instructed him and Woofer on what we were about to do, and how imperative it was to remain in the background. Never look like we were following her. Without much hope of them pulling it off, we nonetheless moved through the park at as discreet a distance as possible.

She crossed the road and headed through the city, ever watchful, but we merged with the endless cyclists and those on horseback, donkey, the carts, and the occasional vehicle delivering to homes and business, so blended in perfectly.

She stopped in a small street lined with cafes and strange new shops selling things I couldn't even begin to guess the purpose of, lots of tech way beyond my interest, and pulled out her phone. She spoke for a few seconds then looked up and laughed as she nodded then waved. I followed her line of sight and my heart froze.

The woman hurried forward to where another was seated at a cafe, sipping a drink. People around her were chatting as they wiped at their brows, even under the large awning. When she arrived, they embraced and smiled warmly at each other then immediately began talking excitedly, as though there was great news. The waiter came and took her order then left; they didn't stop talking the whole time.

Why this? Why now? What should I do? I knew what I should do, but I stayed there, rooted to the spot, gawping. I cursed Liverpool. I cursed myself. I cursed my wife for leaving me and taking my daughter with her all those years ago. Because there was absolutely no doubt about it. This was my daughter, all grown up, clearly having inherited her mother's abilities, maybe mine too. Two witches together, meeting up for a drink. Mother and daughter. My wife, my daughter. Neither of whom I had lain eyes on for over a century.

I took one more glance, then turned Bernard around as angry cyclists shouted at us for getting in the way. I didn't look back, didn't dare, because more than anything I wanted to go over and say hello. Apologize for what I'd done, but to ask why she'd left. Why she had to take the only good thing remaining in my life, and never let me see her again?

What good would it do? It was so long ago; they had a life without me. I was a stranger now. To them, sometimes to myself.

I could never see them again, never talk to them. Too much time had passed, too much bad had happened. I was unable to speak to them because what then? Happy families? Take them home to the new wife and new daughter? No, they had their lives, I had mine. I would not ruin anyone else's.

But it hurt. It hurt so much I felt like my insides were bleeding. I wiped at my eyes, gritted my teeth, and kept going.

I always did. I always would.

I didn't look back. I never looked back.

But I wanted to.

Down Comes the Rain

Thunder cracked overhead; I looked to the sky as black clouds roiled. Rain, beautiful rain, fell in such a torrent it hurt my face. Woofer yelped, Bernard sighed with gratitude as the temperature plummeted, and I sniffled as my tears were washed away. People whooped, whilst others ran for cover. I just sat there on Bernard in the middle of the street, letting him take me where he would.

In seconds I was soaked to the bone. It was a strange feeling. A proper downpour hadn't occurred in summer for years. I couldn't recall the last time it had happened. We got wet winters, way too wet, but spring, summer, and even autumn were seasons as dry as Tyr's insides.

The wyrmling, although I guess he wasn't one any more, called out to me, complaining morosely about the wet and cold even though it was still hot as hell. But the humidity was rising fast, and dragons and water did not mix well. I told him to go take cover somewhere high where there was a good overhang, and promised I'd check in on him later when the storm passed.

We needed to find cover too, so I directed Bernard to seek out somewhere we could all rest up for a while. Bernard moved of his own accord, following a trail only one gifted such as he could read. Through flooded streets, where blocked drains couldn't cope with the volume of water, now almost deserted, he eased into a trot, but it was fast enough to splash water high. Within minutes, he pulled up outside one of the many new businesses opened up to cater to the new way of things. Like an old-fashioned tavern more than anything else, with a large stable block in an adjacent building right in the heart of the city.

Necrosanctuary.

"Not my first choice, Bernard. Can't we go somewhere else?"

"I need this. I am exhausted, and so are you. We need somewhere safe. This is safe."

"Safe? It'll be full of Necros and tourists. You know what they're like about anything with Necro in the name. It's like a game to them. Trying to uncover the mystery of the Necro chain of businesses. Come on, let's find a different place. Last thing I want is to draw even more attention to us all."

"No. This is where we should be."

"Okay, fine, suit yourself. But it better not mean trouble."

I dismounted and led Bernard through a high arch and around the back of the building, where a large courtyard was covered in huge tarps to provide shade. Rain poured down the sides in a series of fast-flowing miniature rivers, but kept the rest of the yard dry. Several stalls in a modified building the other side of the courtyard were occupied, but plenty were empty. A few riders were hanging around by their animals, smoking, drinking beers or teas and coffees, but it seemed quiet enough.

A young lad came over and gave me the usual spiel about what they had to offer. I told him food for the "horse" and for Woofer and me. Plus a beer. If he saw what Bernard really was he didn't let on. A place like this, they would get all sorts, but Bernard was still a real rarity even in a world of Necros. Which was exactly why I didn't like establishments like this. We were not to be trusted. Give us an inch, and we'd take a mile, plus the bloody ruler.

"Bernard, you sure about this?" I asked again once he was in his stable and about to get settled for a few hours of rest.

"Yes. It's safe, it's clean, and it's what we need. Sometimes I know what's best for you."

I nodded and left him to it. It was always weird when he acted like this, almost like he knew what he was doing. Quite unsettling. I preferred it when he broke windows or killed the cat. Things like that were easy to understand and get annoyed by. Him being smart didn't sit well at all.

Inside was like many other pubs, but this place had a ring of magic to it. I hated it immediately. There was a serious underground movement of Necros where they grouped together and acted out all kinds of crap. Happened all over the country, especially in large towns and cities. They'd gather in these naff places, feeling smug and like they were somehow better than everyone else. Telling stories, showing off, reveling in the exclusive club they had been made members of. Certain among us enjoyed the notoriety, the kudos that grew year on year as their kill count rose. They got off on it. It was the one thing nobody could argue with—if you were alive past twenty-one, you'd killed.

By the looks of it, this place was full of jokers like that. Patting each other on the back for being awesome, when there was nothing to be proud of. They were sacrificial pawns in a cosmic game of chess they could never hope to win, and were kidding themselves if they thought any of us were heroes.

As Woofer and I moved to a vacant table with a bench seat up against the wall, and two chairs, the place went quiet. Several heads turned our way and there were a few whispers. This was all I needed. What was Bernard playing at bringing us here? I recognized nobody, but knew word would filter through to other Necros if anyone did know me. I did not want that. I hated being tracked, people knowing my business, and this would pretty much blow my cover. Would my mark hear about this? Would he be warned?

I cursed Bernard again. This was a bad idea. Why had I let him talk me into this?

I nodded to the pretty young waitress as she set my drink down and placed a bowl of water on the grubby floorboards for Woofer. She said she'd return with my food in ten minutes or so. The lass was nervous, stuttered and almost spilled my drink. I drank deeply, then rubbed at my hair and face with a towel she'd kindly provided. The room was still quiet, but slowly people were returning to their conversations or nursing their drinks. Several regular people were here too, but the majority were definitely Necros. I could tell, same as they could.

I hardly noticed my soaked clothes as I sat there sipping my beer without even tasting it. My head was spinning. Why was it everywhere I went there was something to haunt me? To sidetrack me from what I had to do? It was almost like I was being tested. Pushed to my limits to see what would make me snap. Maybe they knew they'd be here, and this was why I had been sent out of my usual zone? Given a job that should have gone to someone else because they knew I would see my previous wife and daughter. Could that be true? And why? It made sense though. I only had to look around to be sure there were plenty of others who could have been given this job.

To screw with me, that was why I'd been chosen. Push and push and push until I broke. I would bend, but I would never break. I was beyond that now. Maybe I was cold. Was that why I knew deep down that I could deal with this? It's hard to analyze yourself in such detail; we want to believe we are a good, caring person. What if that isn't true? I had these doubts. I had concerns over my emotional stability, worried I was insane, cruel, unworthy of what I had. But I knew I loved deeply, had always loved with intensity, and yet here I was, letting go of a past I'd thought I'd finished with, because... Why? Why didn't I go and say hello? Fear of rejection? Fear of acceptance? Fear of the unknown?

Fear of myself? What I might do?

It was because she had left, and too much time had passed. I was not part of that family any more. I had been shunned, but that wasn't my daughter's fault, was it? All I knew was I could not speak to them. I was in a good place with a perfect family of my own once more, and it had taken longer than an average lifetime to recover sufficiently before I was ready for it to happen. And however much I had loved my previous families, I was honest enough with myself to admit that I had never loved with the intensity I did now. Was that bad? Was it even true? In a hundred years' time, would I be able to pass Jen and Phage by, no matter what had happened in the past? I didn't think so, but how did I know?

After such introspection I came to one conclusion. I was being fucked with. The senders of the notes knew this encounter would happen, maybe even arranged it, and it was done to test my resolve. To see how I would react, and watch me unravel. Maybe even lose the confrontation that awaited. Was that it? A way to eradicate me?

"Stop fucking thinking, Soph," I grumbled to myself. It did no good, this never-ending circle of questions. My mind was like the spinning wheel on my phone when the signal was iffy. Round and round, getting nowhere. I had a job to do, so I'd get it done then return home and continue with my life.

How I missed Phage. How I longed to see Jen's smile. To wander into her room and feel bewildered by all the trappings of the modern world, even one in such turmoil. I wanted to be confused by her music, dazzled by her prowess with computers, and tell her she was absolutely not going out dressed like that.

I smiled. I would get through this.

When I looked up and came back to the present, it was to find I had finished my beer and my food was set in front of me. I looked around the room and caught the eye of the waitress. I nodded my thanks and smiled. She beamed back shyly, as though I was a rock star and made her nervous. More likely, I made her anxious by not acknowledging her when she brought my food.

But as I took in the room properly for the first time, it was clear she wasn't the only one. Several Necros were watching me closely, as though I might do something interesting. I had no intention of doing anything but eating my food and getting the hell out of here. How long did I have left? Days. I was fine. No hurry. Maybe I should get a room and rest up for the night? Have a fresh start in the morning. It might even stop raining. Rain. It seemed weird.

I glared back at anyone blatantly staring, until they turned away. What was their problem? Feeling like a specimen on show, and I didn't know why, I tucked into my late lunch with gusto. Damn, I was starving. All the stress of fighting, I guess. Ah, the fight. Did everyone know? Was that it? Had the word got out about Tyr and the mad Necro riding a unicorn?

"Woofer feel funny."

"What's up?" I asked him, checking this was a purely mental conversation.

"People staring. Talking about us."

"What are they saying?" I asked, intrigued.

"Don't know, too quiet. But they keep looking."

I patted his head and told him, "Just ignore them. Want a sausage?"

Woofer's head snapped up and he panted, tail brushing the floor. "Love sausage!"

I caught the waitress' eye and called, "Can we have a heap of sausages for my friend here?" She smiled timidly then hurried back into the kitchen.

"Won't be long," I told him. "Just ignore everyone and dream of sausages." A long line of drool hung from his mouth as he did exactly that. I laughed loudly, surprising myself and several customers. What was with me? Stress, I told myself. I was stressed, and rightly so.

I continued with my sausage, egg, chips, and beans. Focused on my plate, and ignored the surreptitious looks boring into my soul. Was it because I was wet? The dog? It was getting on my nerves. The waitress hurried over with a massive bowl full of sausages and I said, "Can you put them down for the dog, please?"

"Y...yes. S...sure. Here you go, boy." She placed them next to Woofer and he looked up at me. I nodded. He didn't need telling twice.

"Sorry, excuse me," I said as she went to leave.

"Yes?" She fidgeted with her apron, wringing it out like a wet towel.

"Do you know why everyone's looking at me? It's freaking me out."

"It's... Nothing. Not my place, sir."

"No, it's fine. Honestly. I won't be mad or anything. I'm feeling self-conscious here."

"Well, they say you're Necrosoph. Is that right, sir?" She looked panicked; she was ready to run.

"Soph's the name, yeah. But how does anyone know? How do they all know? How do you know me?"

"Stands to reason, doesn't it? It's you. Necrosoph."

"Yes, you said that." I tried to remain calm, but I could tell I was upsetting her. "Sorry, don't be scared. I mean, how do you know me? Any of you?"

"Because everyone knows your name. At least around here. It's from before, way before my time. Don't you remember? They all do, the old-timers. No offense, sir. They're always telling the stories. You know what other Necros are like. Love a tall tale. They told the one about you and the warlock. Happened just a town over. The chatty ones, they say it was you, Soph, and they say you look the same. It's true, isn't it?"

"Yeah, I guess. But it's nothing noble. Nothing to talk about really. You don't talk about notes, you know that."

She looked at me, puzzled. "I know that, sir. None of us do. Oh no, never say a word. It wasn't a note, was it? They never said. The stories they tell, it was a fight, plain and simple. Not a note job. No, sir, we never talk about the notes. That's against the rules, that is." She looked at me quizzically then scampered, bowing like I was royalty as she backed away.

At least now I knew why I was getting the funny looks. Guess my good looks and badass moves had preceded me, at least in this corner of Blighty.

If only I could recall the event properly. She said it wasn't a note. Maybe it wasn't. This was the problem with so much killing—it all blurred. You got to a point where you blamed everything on the notes, when sometimes it was either a fight before or after the main event. I recalled the warlock, I'd fought a few in my time, but the details were hazy. There was a crowd somehow, but beyond that it was just a distant, forgotten memory.

I wasn't about to ask anyone. I didn't want to know, but what I did know was I didn't like being the focus of the room. A low profile was better, not for every dim-witted Necro in a hundred-mile radius to know an old man with a penchant for slippers and an afternoon snooze was roaming the city. That was not being a Necroninja. It was being a Necrotwat.

I finished my food then placed my cutlery neatly on the plate and sighed as I leaned back. Woofer had finished long ago, and was sitting there staring at me, vibing the sausage machine to get a move on and refill the bowl.

"Haha, that's all you're getting, you greedy bugger." Woofer's ears flattened. He'd live.

Damn, I was beat. I could curl up and sleep right here if it wasn't for all these eyes on me.

I began to drift off, but the squeal of a chair being dragged back on the floor made me force my eyes to open. I could smell trouble. A big guy with numerous piercings and a chiseled jaw was grinning at me as he sauntered over. Everyone watched.

I held up my hand. He stopped. "No, I'm not him. No, I don't want to talk. No, I'm not joking."

He frowned, then cracked a cocky smile and kept on coming. He pulled out a chair and sat down, uninvited. The dimwit sat on it backwards, a manly straddle like it made him more Alpha. Utter fuckwit move.

"You're him. I knew it! Man, the stories I've heard about you and some of the other old-timers. Not about notes, of course," he said hurriedly, looking around nervously, "but, you know, other stuff."

"I don't want to talk. I just said. I explicitly said I was not joking. I didn't ask you to sit. Please leave."

He grinned at me. How the fuck had he lived long enough to grow his hair? Guys this stupid died before they got past thinking they were men, when really they were boys. "I don't take any crap either." He flexed his chest muscles. I flexed my jaw.

"Yeah, I bet."

"You trying to be funny? Was that an insult?" He glared at me, his hackles up at the slight he thought he'd received. I sighed, then I leaned forward, smiling, and beckoned him closer. Grinning like the utter dipshit he undoubtedly was, he moved towards me. I grabbed his hair, slammed his head so hard on the table the wood cracked, and he nearly snapped his neck as his throat caught on the back of the chair, then shoved him back. He toppled over and lay there, out cold. A large angry lump popped up on his forehead, and he had a vicious purple bruise right across his throat. I wiped my hands on wet jeans to try to remove the greasy product from his hair.

Everyone in the room applauded. Two youngsters came over, all gangly nerves, and dragged him away after I nodded permission. I gave another nod to the appreciative clientele then closed my eyes. Nobody else bothered me.

Nice one, Soph, I told myself, way to keep a low profile.

I woke up with a jump, to find the nervous waitress standing over me.

"Sorry, did you say something?"

"Y... yes. Um, we're closing. On account of the electric. We open up again later, but it's mostly candles then. S... sorry."

"Hey, no problem. I'm the one who should be apologizing. Let me pay. Sorry for holding you up." I reached for my wallet to get my card, but she put her tiny, pale hand nervously over mine.

"It's on the house. My treat. Um, well, haha, actually it's the owner's treat. He does the cooking, saw what happened. Knew the stories about you too. The... the others have left. Just me here now." She smiled shyly, but her body language told another story. "I just have to lock up. I live upstairs. Alone. The owner goes home to his family when it's closing time. Just us now." She smiled, eyes locking on mine.

"That's very sweet, and you are a lovely girl, but I'm married. I hope that means something to you."

"Oh, gosh. No, they didn't say. They said you were single. S... sorry, I would never, you know, if I knew you were..." She fiddled with her apron again, then clearly felt brave and said, "That's so sweet, that you're faithful. I hope I get a man like that one day."

"I have no doubt you will. Can I give you bit of advice? And by the way, I am very flattered. I'm not exactly a catch at the moment."

"You look lovely. Very handsome. But it's not that, it's... Well, it's how you are. You didn't do that to the man earlier to impress. You did what you knew had to be done and you didn't wait, let it turn into a brawl. You acted first, did what would solve the problem with the least trouble. I like that. Gosh, I sound so silly. I'm not normally such a fangirl, honest."

"Haha, I believe you. And wow, thank you. Now, that advice. When you find a good man, hold on to him. Treat him well, make sure he treats you even better. And never, ever, let him talk down to you or treat you like anything other than a princess. Because that's what you are. I know some of these guys, the way they act. It's all a front. They're scared deep down, and that's okay, but when you're alone with them, no matter the show they put on for others, you just make sure they treat you like you deserve. You got all that?"

She nodded seriously. "You're a nice man. Thank you. And sorry, for earlier."

"Hey, nothing to apologize for. My ego can never get too big for compliments from gorgeous young women. You take care." I got up, gathered my gear, then called Woofer and we went out into the courtyard. I heard the lock click behind me.

The compliment was nice, very nice, but now it meant I couldn't stay here for the night. I sorted out a deal with the lad in charge of the stables, then went where he directed me and found myself in a cheap, grubby room just around the corner. It was quiet, there was a bed, and I got right down to the serious business of oblivion.

I woke up the following day, after a dreamless sleep, with Woofer lying on the pillow next to me. When I opened my eyes, he licked my eyeball.

My head throbbed. I needed water. The grimy bathroom was not to be trusted, and neither was the water, so I just showered quickly, sluicing away the grime of yesterday and probably the day before, brushed my teeth, did all the other things a man does in the morning, then dressed in dry clothes. Yesterday's were still somewhat damp, so I balled them up, put them in a reusable bag, and stuffed it all into the bowels of my pack. It would be a nice surprise when I got home.

After getting myself together, and my head in the right place, I checked the location on my phone then left the crummy "hotel" and went to get Bernard. The rain had stopped, leaving Liverpool glistening like a mirage.

Humidity was through the roof, and I was drenched before I trudged halfway there.

New Levels of Stupid

"You took your time," griped Bernard, as he glared at me with his darling pale blue eyes.

"And you got fat. Look at your bloody stomach. What have they been feeding you, balloons?"

"I'll have you know I'm watching my weight. I might have had a trickle of molasses with my feed, but only because the nice young man looking after me, unlike some, was a fan."

"Of what, fat unicorns with math problems? And you might be watching your weight, but you're watching it go in the wrong direction, buddy."

"I can do math. Um, what's math? Is it like sums? I can do sums."

"Woofer good at sums. Soph play ball? Woofer can count to one. One." My adorable dog wagged his tail. He didn't have a clue, poor guy.

"Yes, well done, smart dog, you counted to one." He wagged again. My awesome jokes were lost on this pair.

"Okay, I'm gonna settle up then we can get going. This is the big day, so let's be on our best form. Any trouble, you two scarper. Do as I ask, and we'll be fine. Any problems while I was away?" I asked Bernard.

"Is this a problem?" he asked. He moved sheepishly away from the pile of straw in the corner of the stable to reveal an upturned, and very large, jug of molasses. Needless to say, it was as empty as his skull.

"Hell, no wonder you look like an elephant about to give birth. Tell me you knocked it over. Do not tell me you ate the lot."

"I knocked it over."

"Phew, that's a relief. Because if you ate, or is it drank, all that, you'd be exploding liquid shit soon enough."

"And then I ate it all. It's definitely ate. I chewed it."

"Then you're more inept than I gave you credit for," I told him. "Well done."

"Thank you. What's inept?"

"You are."

Faaarp.

Woofer and I jumped back as a noxious stench pinged around the stable in an utter panic, searching for a fast escape from its own foulness. The molecular malfeasance reached terminal velocity, vaulted over the half-open stable door, then clung to me, bewildered and afraid, terrified by its own sudden creation.

I coughed and spluttered and batted at my clothes; Woofer ran and hid.

"Hell, that is not possible. That smell cannot, must not, be a thing. It's sentient!" I screamed. A deep nose-sweat threatened to make me breathe, which would be a very bad thing, then my ears began pouring salty water, like that would help. I doubled over and dry-heaved.

"Oh no, I think I feel unwell." Bernard, fear in his eyes, circled the stall, trying to escape his own misery.

"Call me when it's over. Should only take an hour or so to evacuate your idiocy," I hollered jovially, as I hightailed it out of there and went to find somewhere for breakfast while Bernard got what he deserved.

"This is nice," I told my less stinky companion as we sat outside a lovely little cafe and people-watched while I enjoyed a fry-up and he enjoyed watching me eat it. He'd already inhaled his, of course; I would never leave him hungry like that.

Citizens were out in force, having believed the rain would have cooled things down. It had made things worse. The sun was now out for revenge. It was up early, in full battle regalia. Its enemy? People. It's one goal? Burn, burn, and if not, then at least a slow frazzle.

Even under the requisite canopy, I was feeling queasy from the excessive moisture, and I was sure I could smell Bernard's foul extrusions. It had followed me, wound its way through streets then insinuated itself in my nostrils and decide to have a doze. I gulped crappy coffee to try to eradicate the taste. Even the best baristas had to make do with dodgy beans these days, and I got the sneaking suspicion this wasn't even real beans, just some concoction a lazy scientist had put together when feeling especially vindictive. I drank it anyway, hoping it contained dangerous levels of caffeine, synthetic or otherwise.

Drones were thin on the ground. Maybe the moisture was playing with their electronic insides. Nobody gave us a second glance, and it suited me perfectly. I knew I should be in hiding, I absolutely did not want to meet the women of my past life, but somehow I knew that was done with. I wouldn't see them now.

I called out to Tyr, who had been quiet. He would be resting, as it was what he did most of the time nowadays. Any form of excitement made him crash out for hours, just like a young child coming down after an all-day playdate with unlimited sweets. So after yesterday's insanity, I wouldn't be surprised if he was out for days, if not weeks. Tough. He'd have to suck it up. Hopefully, we'd be on our way home tomorrow, maybe even later today. It was only Tuesday, and that gave me cheer.

Tyr was slow to respond, still sleeping, so I called again and he woke, mind slow, and not very communicative.

"Tyr, I have a few things to sort out, so hang low. You still out of sight?"

"Very tired. Feel strange." There was a pause. He was confused. "Tyr's body large. Looks funny. I'm too big."

"That's because you fed yesterday. Do you remember?"

"Remember. Very tired. Sleep more." He yawned, then I received a mental image of his eyes closing and his mind shutting down.

"It's alright for some," I muttered.

We got our things together, meaning, I got my things together and Woofer sat next to an elderly couple and did the, "I've never been fed in my life, and Labrador's need feeding," routine. They caved, and he snagged a few chips. Weirdly, they were eating fish and chips for breakfast! Takes all sorts. I apologized to them for Woofer's behavior, but they were cool.

I told Woofer to stop begging, then went inside and paid for my breakfast and the nice couple's too. The woman behind the counter smiled at me. Damn, they sure were friendly around here. Or was it just that I never usually saw anyone unless they had a knife poking out of their eye? That was a surefire way to kill the mood.

Back outside, I smiled at the couple as the man gave woofer a few more chips, and we headed back to laugh at Bernard for being a greedy unicorn. We should have waited another hour.

One Man and His Dog

"Bloody hell, Bernard, look at the state of you."

"I don't feel well," he groaned.

"Woofer not like smell, and Woofer like smell of other dog's bums."

"Yeah, he absolutely reeks. You hear that, Bernard? Even Woofer thinks you stink. It's gross."

"Ugh, I need to lie down." Bernard turned several times, found a clean corner of the stable, and plonked himself onto the straw with a sigh. He looked like a shiny turtle. His legs poked out funny from his bloated stomach because he couldn't lie comfortably with it in the way.

The stall wasn't as messy as I'd expected, so I suspected the lad had been and reluctantly cleaned out the worst of the mess already. The empty jar was also gone.

"This will teach you to stop being so greedy," I lectured. "You'll have to stay here while we get about our business. When we're done, I'll come back and get you. If I don't return, then just do your unicorn stuff and find your way home. I'm not calling Phage now to tell her you're in a mess, she'll worry. Although I do need to message her," I recalled.

"Don't be long. I want to go home," he moaned.

"I'll be as quick as I can. Remember to drink lots of water, that'll settle you. And do not eat anything!"

"Ugh, I won't. I'm never eating molasses again."

"Oh, right, you mean like the other month when you did this exact same thing when Jen left the container out and you accidentally knocked it over, got the lid off, and licked the bottle clean? How is that even a thing? The opening is smaller than your tongue."

"It was an accident," he whined.

"You've got nobody to blame but yourself. You should know better. Rest up, we'll see you later."

Woofer waited while I went and got the lad. He was tending horses in the block across the yard and looked knackered already.

"Keeping you busy?"

"Yeah, bleedin' nightmare. That creature of yours is a bit dim, isn't he? Um, no offense."

"He's won awards. Not that he remembered to collect his medals."

He frowned at me. "I don't get it."

I slapped him playfully across the back. "Don't sweat it. Look, thanks for looking after him. Just be careful with the sweet treats, okay?"

"I will. They'll take it out of my pay."

"You look after Bernard, I'll be back late tonight or maybe tomorrow. Pass me your card reader. You got a way to get a tip?"

"Yeah, sure." He brightened instantly.

"Let me pay up until tomorrow, and then do your thing so I can give you a little extra."

He sorted out the reader and I gave him a generous tip so Bernard would be in good hands. He stared at the number and said, "Cool. Thanks, mister. Hear you had some bother inside yesterday. Don't mind those guys, they just like to natter. Right gossips, the lot of them."

"Yeah, I just wanted a quiet place for a few hours. It is what it is."

"Haha, you should see the lump on Pete's head. He wasn't happy."

"He was a dick. I was in a bad mood." I shrugged it off. I had more important things to worry about.

"He is. Anyway, thanks."

"No problem. Just take care of the idiot horse."

"I will. He's a fine 'horse', that one. Wish I had one like him." He winked.

I nodded that I understood. "Just keep him out of sight if you know how special he is. I don't want anyone trying to take him. Not that he'd let them. He's family. Understand?"

"Gotcha."

"Oh, my pack's in there with him. I hung it up. I've got my valuables, but I'd hate for it to go missing." I patted the small pack on my back, so he understood anything worth stealing was off-limits, but it felt rude doing so.

"Don't worry. We run a respectable place."

"I'm sure you do. Sorry, just being paranoid."

I left him to his work, and called Woofer. Bernard snored loudly in the fetid stall.

"Just you and me, Woofer. This is what you wanted, right? An adventure with me? How's it been so far?"

"Woofer like being with Soph. Doesn't like city. Smelly and busy. Want grass and trees and somewhere to play." I saw the cogs working. "Play ball with Woofer?"

"Not now, but when this is over we can play ball all the way home. How does that sound?"

He wagged excitedly. Oh, how I wished my life was as simple as his.

Right, I'd screwed around enough here. I had to get this over with. My guts tightened, my heart beat fast. It was time to kill.

We walked through the main thoroughfares of the city; no way was I going anywhere quiet unless necessary. I did not want a repeat of yesterday. We slowly made our way north-east, heading towards the location I'd been given. I messaged Phage as we walked; she was fine. Jen was fine too. They both missed me. I missed them too, I told her. I got a smiley face in return. I tried to send one back, but fluffed it and sent a turd instead. She sent a shocked smiley face right back at me. I sent an oops and a haha. Seemed the safer bet.

Smiling, my spirits lifted by connecting with my wife, I walked for an hour past houses and ancient buildings, the solitude welcome. Woofer kept silent and walked close to me. He was not a city boy. Carts full of produce trundled past. There were a surprising number of smart carriages, one of the few booming businesses of recent years, and I marveled at the contraptions people used to get about here. I even saw a Sinclair c5, and endless variations of bicycles with weird configurations. The sights of human ingenuity lifted my spirits.

The humidity had dropped as the rain evaporated, so I didn't feel like I was wading through a bath of warm water any more, but the city was cloying. No air flow, I assumed. Too built-up. Narrow streets and high skyscrapers, tower blocks everywhere you looked. It was one such tower block I was heading towards.

It was a sea of concrete where we were headed. Early eighties city planning gone horribly wrong. I was amazed it still stood; most of these buildings had been razed long ago, replaced with something more hospitable. They were magnets for gangs, and crime was usually high. You only had to look at the endless expanse of inferior concrete to understand why.

But I was proven utterly wrong as we moved from the shade of a broad, tree-lined street into the vast swathe of man-made hostility. Brightly colored awnings, canopies, gazebos and more dotted the area. People had cobbled together swings and climbing frames and things for the kids to play on, and groups of people hung out laughing, watching children of all ages run around like nutters. It was a heart-warming sight.

We ambled across the area as though we belonged, heading straight for a walkway that curved around the darkest recesses and up several levels to the main entrance to the block. It must have only been fifteen stories, but it felt huge, looming like the dead carcass of a stranded alien creature with strange spindly protrusions near the roof.

Drones buzzed frantically overhead. Watching everything. Watching me.

Dead eyes followed our ascent. Large rectangles of glass where no lights shone.

You needed a code or keycard to get in, so I did a quick morph, sucked up the pain for such a ridiculously short trip, and came back to myself the other side of the glass door. I doubled over, sweating, my hunger already rising.

I pushed open the door for Woofer, then moved to the side of the very clean lobby and crouched down to speak to him.

"I want you to stay here. I need to go up very high and I know for a fact you'll hate the elevator. I don't know what I'm going to find, so best you wait here. Guard the entrance for me, boy. Make sure nobody comes up that looks like they would hurt me. Can you do that?"

"Woofer likes elevators."

"No, you don't. And this is an important job. You're the guard. Okay?"

He did the puppy dog act, but I was hardened to it so only felt awful for a few seconds. I patted his head, reminded him again what he had to do, then went over to the elevator and pressed the button for the top floor.

This was it. Crunch time.

Determined not to break the tradition of every person ever who has used an elevator, I punched the button again, even though it was clearly already on its way down. It pinged as it stuttered to a shaky halt, and the doors opened. There were no mirrors, no cool light effects, just torn stickers advertising select entertainment. But it was clean—the residents clearly cared about their home.

I saluted Woofer as the doors closed and my juddering ascent began. Ah. Alone for what felt like the first time in days. I preferred being alone. Nobody to see the cruelty hiding within. The floor shuddered and something grated horribly, but then the doors slid back reluctantly. I exited onto a balcony that wrapped around the building, maybe six feet wide. It was covered in grimy perspex, chewed through in places by weather never envisioned. Running along the left side were nondescript doors to people's homes.

Once again, I thanked my lucky stars for my home. I'd go mad living here. It wasn't a judgement. I'd spent time in cities and enjoyed it. You had parks, pubs, cinemas, and all manner of places to eat. But I'd always felt confined, a stranger. Alone when surrounded by too many people. I needed grass and forests and flowers. Somewhere I could scream without being carted off for extended supervision by head doctors.

I checked my phone. The location was always extremely accurate nowadays, so I looked along the balcony then back to the map and figured it was the seventh door. Maybe the eighth. Who could live here that was such a threat? It could have been anyone, for any number of reasons. Or it could be someone who didn't need to die. That happened too. Not as often as I liked, but it did happen. It was a matter of judgement, my call, and I dared not get it wrong.

The seventh door was marked with polished brass numbers. The door was green, freshly painted, with a matching letterbox, and a white plastic doorbell. The button was clean, like it had never been used. Outside was an umbrella, a pair of old boots, and a mat with 'Welcome' stamped in cheery letters. I checked the doors either side. Maybe it was one of those?

To the left was another matching door, but with stickers plastered all over the insides of the windows. Doubtful it was that one, but it could be. To the right was a door that'd seen better days. The bell was gone, the paint peeling, the umbrella leaning against the wall was torn. The windows were filthy, and the letterbox was sealed shut, which made sense—they wouldn't have had mail delivered up here for decades as there were mail slots down in the lobby. But something else told me it wasn't this door. The vibe was wrong. This was an elderly person scraping by. It had nets at the windows; people didn't use them now. The other properties had blinds. I peered through all three in turn; each gave limited views of cramped kitchens. The one to the right was old-fashioned beyond belief, the left was dated, full of cereal boxes and snacks on the counter. The middle one had simple but modern cupboards, a nice tap, and the counter and sink were spotless.

It was this door.

I went about my business in the usual fashion. I didn't think about it. Didn't second-guess my decisions. I sure as hell didn't try to be smart.

Without a better plan, I rang the bell. I'd learned over the years that trying to batter down doors or morphing into the unknown was often the worst choice. Better for them to open up, so I could get a feel for things, before I did something stupid.

Plus, of course, it might be the wrong property. Don't want to appear in someone's living room and terrify the kids or make a baby cry. Or interrupt some afternoon sexy times. It was nigh on impossible to morph anyway, even at a close distance, if I couldn't picture exactly where I wanted to be.

Already tired from getting through the door downstairs, I waited patiently and tried to still my hammering heart.

Bloody Wizards

Footsteps squeaked along what sounded like a tiled hallway. They were slow and cautious. Understandable, as I doubted there were many callers to the folks up here.

"Hello?" called a man from the other side of the door.

"Hi," I called back brightly. "I just moved in on the next floor down. Blimey, that was no fun getting everything up here. Anyway, haha, you don't need to hear about that. I tried a bunch of other doors, but no one's answering. I know this sounds stupid, but you couldn't lend me some milk, could you? I'm dying here. I need my cup of tea before I even start sorting my new place out. It's a rough mess."

"Milk?"

"Yes. Help me out, please? I'm dying for a cuppa. Managed to find my kettle and tea bags, but no milk. Sorry to trouble you. I'll return the favor, honest."

"Hang on." I heard him shuffling about then a few bangs. He returned and the Yale lock was released. The door opened and I was confronted with a man who looked not a day over twenty-five. But looks could be deceiving. He had short dark hair in a modern style, shiny with gel or something, pristine, well-groomed stubble, and a handsome face. He wore loungewear. A tracksuit thing with weird baggy bits then tight at the ankles—I assumed it was fashionable, but I could have been wrong. It certainly didn't look it to my jaded eyes.

All of this was taken in and assimilated in a moment. As he studied me, presumably in a similar fashion, he was already handing over a half-empty glass bottle of milk.

"Here. Just bring the empty back. I have to use it for a refill."

"Sure," I said, smiling. I lifted my head and we locked eyes.

"Shit," he hissed. The milk dropped from his hands, the bottle smashed on the threshold, and he gripped the door and tried to slam it.

"Sorry, don't think so." I shoved the door back at him and it smacked into his head. He yelped, then ran back inside and slammed a door shut to what I assumed was the living room at the far end of the hallway.

I kicked the glass away from the door, then closed and locked it before I eased vigilantly along the hallway. I tried the handle, but it was locked from the inside. This guy was clearly expecting trouble, but human nature still takes over.

He would help a neighbor, so did that mean he was a good guy? Or someone not wanting to reveal their true nature? Even psychopaths will lend you milk. They might kill you if you don't return the bottle, but still.

"Go away," the man shouted. "I know who you are. Don't hurt me."

"Who are you?" I called back, not unkindly.

"Fuck! You don't even know, do you? Course you don't. Look, I'm nobody, just leave me alone. Go away. I'm just a guy getting started. Don't hurt me, please."

"Open the door and let's have a chat. You know how this works. It doesn't mean I have to kill you. Open up. Convince me." I put my ear to the door and listened. It had gone quiet.

I felt the air vibrate behind me and hurled myself at the side wall as the man thrust out with a knife even as he was solidifying. With his arm extended, I grabbed him at the elbow and smashed his forearm onto my rising knee. He was good, knew the drill, and twisted as I yanked down, the knife angle changing so it bit deeply into the side of my leg.

He punched me in the kidneys with his free hand and kneed me repeatedly anywhere he could. I countered with an old favorite, the head-butt, and as his vision blurred and his attack slowed, I shoved him back against the opposite wall in the cramped hall and gripped my own knife tightly.

"You fucking idiot," he spat. "You think I'm a dumb kid? I've been waiting for you."

"You didn't have much of a plan then," I told him.

"No?" he cackled, as he morphed. I heard him stumble in the living room, so I put my shoulder to the door and smashed through the flimsy material, busting the lock out of the cheap wooden frame.

As I tumbled into the room, I knew I was screwed. Fast as I was able, I morphed, the rending of my body unbearable as the world became pure pain, but it wasn't a moment too soon. The gunfire echoed around the room and I felt the bullet go through my disparate midsection. It hurt like a bitch, but I knew I'd live. The feeling was so bizarre. I'd been shot before, and it hurt just as badly, but I wasn't physically harmed.

I solidified right behind him and stabbed into his kidney, but the blade stopped dead. A fucking vest. He sure did expect someone to come at some point. Why?

I skipped back as he turned and tried to fire, but I dove low before the gun was up and we tumbled back into a chair, the only piece of furniture in the room. The gun went off, but it did nothing but ruin the plastered ceiling. He struggled as I tried to get an arm free to end this, but he shucked and squirmed, then bit deep into my shoulder. I gritted my teeth and bore the pain, but we were a mess of limbs, neither of us getting anywhere. And then the true madness surfaced. The erasure of emotion, nothing but the fight I would not lose. Losing is the dead guy's business.

Consumed, my years of fighting took over and I went nuts on the guy. A full-on frenzy. I bit back, I punched and stabbed and hit and tore but he kept gripping me tight, strong way beyond his size should allow. And when my vision cleared enough to understand why, it was obvious.

He was bloody well gone.

I'd been kicking the shit out of the chair. It was in tatters. Cushions were torn to shreds, the wooden arms covered in bite marks, a sorry scene of deranged madness.

Gasping, I clambered out of the cloud of filling and turned, ready for anything. There was nothing but silence.

Time for some snooping. I didn't really even have to leave the chair. This place was not what it appeared in the slightest. The room contained a chair, a rug, and a laptop. There was a large power bank supplying it, and a mains lead too. He clearly needed electricity and ensured he always had plenty to spare. But he'd left the device behind. I dismissed it. It would be password-protected and of no use.

What interested me more was the absence of stuff. He didn't live here, at least not on even a semi-permanent basis. He came here, sure, but this was not his home. Of that I was now convinced. I'd seen many such places, where people acted out regular-seeming lives but lived anything but. They came and went just enough to make it seem like they were normal, but they spent their lives doing things their neighbors would never understand, never accept.

And he wasn't a young man; I saw that in his eyes. He was old, probably much older than me. Meaning, he moved every few years. Appearing to be that young made it a necessity—you could spend a lot more time in one place when you looked as grizzled as me.

I slumped into the ruined chair and got my breath back. A spring poked into my sore coccyx.

Knowing being thorough was always sensible, I checked through the other rooms. The fridge had basic provisions, cupboards the same. His bathroom was functional. The bedroom had a bed, a few changes of clothes, nothing personal at all. Just a place to receive mail and act regular for when needed. So where was he?

I stepped back out onto the balcony and called to Tyr. He was groggy and uncommunicative; I missed the old wyrmling already.

"Time to earn your keep," I told him.

"Tyr needs to sleep and grow," he moaned.

"You can do that later. I need your help. Now." I described the man, gave a mental picture to Tyr, and tried to imprint his essence on my imagery. It was enough for Tyr to know exactly what I was looking for. Chances were slim he'd find the guy, but it was worth a shot.

I went back inside and rummaged around more, taking it slow this time. I checked every shelf, under every item, in the cupboards, banged the walls, the ceilings, even tore the soap in half and emptied the absolutely ancient shampoo bottles. Nada.

"He's outside the door," came the lazy words of Tyr.

It took a moment for me to process them, and by then it was too late. "What? Here?"

"Yes."

And then the connection was severed.

Whispers crept through the air. Tendrils wrapped around my mind and body, trapping me as I attempted to run. I felt myself become something else, something dying. This was what it felt like to die. I'd experienced it before, and I knew my time was short.

He was a fucking sorcerer. It all clicked into place. This whole thing was a setup. He knew I was coming, he knew when, and he knew what I'd do.

"Bugger. Fucking sorcerers. Reading your bloody mind." He was playing with me. Having a little fun. This man could anticipate the next move, and many more down the line, like a rigged game. He probably holed up here just for me, nothing to do with looking like a regular guy. This wasn't a permanent address; this was not him.

"Sorcerers and their bloody freaky ways." That's why this whole arrangement felt misplaced. He'd just played along, knew if he did certain things what the outcome would be. Knew he'd escape, so why not go with it if it meant he triumphed? After all, if he knew he'd survive, he had the chance to try to kill me. But he'd have seen that too, although it got sketchy about the details. They knew things, saw things, but it was never the same as knowing the future with one hundred percent certainty. Why was he on my note though?

I tried to morph, but his whispers dragged me down, gnawed away at my innate abilities, and much as I struggled I couldn't quite get myself to dissipate. I was wrapped up tighter than a mummy in a bandage shop, and his power got stronger the weaker I became.

Finding myself on my knees, valuable moments lost to darkness, I struggled to my feet and whacked my head into the wall. His hold loosened as my mind lost focus because of the pain. It was enough, and I let a different hurt envelop me and morphed the moment I was able. It wasn't far, I didn't want to get distance, but it worked. His cruel whispers blew away on the air as I materialized behind him and thrust my knife into his stupid bloody tracksuit leg.

"You dare!" he hissed, as he turned and grabbed me in a hell of a bear hug.

I jabbed with my knife but all I hit was his vest. Knowing I had little to lose, but everything to gain, I grinned as I clamped my arms around him, locked my hands together, and shuffled forward, forcing him back as fast as I could manage. Confusion passed over his face, then concern as I nodded at him. Oh yes, I knew exactly what I was doing. His grip already loose, he attempted to squirm free, battering me, shouting, eyes utterly panicked. Guess he hadn't seen this one coming. I merely held on tighter, grunted, and pushed harder with my feet. He hit the balcony, I heaved, and with our bodies locked, we launched over the balcony, fifteen stories above the concrete sea.

"Tyr burn man?"

"No, you'll get me too, and there are people around. Get away, hide. Go invisible, but do not breathe fire near these people."

As I spoke, so I struggled to turn so he was beneath me. His mind was a jumble of conflicting emotions. He wanted me dead, but knew we'd both die if this continued.

From start to finish this took less than a second, much less, and no sooner had I spoken to Tyr than the sorcerer morphed. I maintained my hold on him as I morphed too. Where he went, I went. No escape.

We materialized in a dangerous heap of crimes against physics on short green grass. The sun beat down, the air was heavily perfumed, and all around were roses and hardy flowers in full bloom, defying the heat and putting on a glorious display. Not that there was any time to smell the roses. I had a sorcerer on my back. Literally.

We were both exhausted now. The pain, the terrible agony of morphing had taken nearly all our strength. I nonetheless stabbed out with what energy remained, but just caught his vest again. Once more into the leg, a grunt and a squeal my reward.

He elbowed me in the face, tearing open my lip, then scampered away and sat, panting, watching me intently.

"I see you. I see your actions. I know the moves you will make."

"Bollocks. You didn't know I'd jump off the balcony. That was too stupid for you to know."

He nodded his head. "You are a fool to come after me. I know you, read you. You will lose."

"Don't think so, buddy. I see you too, and I don't know why, but you're bad news. You got anything to say before I kill you?"

"Nothing. The Necronotes come for us all. This is not the first time, but I endure same as the notes. They are testing me, but they want me to live. I am special."

"Yeah, real snowflake. But you got it wrong, sorcerer. I'm here to tell you that. And I will not die. You see that, don't you? You know. Go ahead, take a real good look. I will beat you. I will not die."

I believed it with every ounce of my being. Pure conviction.

He looked nervous as he got awkwardly to his feet. His leg bled profusely but he ignored it. "We shall see. Come, follow me if you dare." He limped off towards a compact stone house at the edge of what I now realized was a garden. Where were we? It couldn't have been far. I would have known if I'd traveled more than a few miles.

I stood, felt his whispers try to force themselves on me, but he was too far away, and weakened by the fight. His magic was nothing but an annoyance, at least for now while he got his act together. Dreaming of a tea break, I pushed the damn whispers away, felt them dissolve into nothing.

The garden was compact and obsessively maintained, edged by a low wall that enclosed a verdant expanse of grass with narrow borders. A stone's throw away was a simple, stout church. I knew this place. I had been here once before. No way was this a coincidence. Headstones glistened through the dappled shade of mature trees.

We were in the vicarage of a small, secluded churchyard, complete with cemetery. Drama queen or what?

Was he the bloody vicar? You couldn't kill vicars. Could you?

Necro Meh

"Shit, Woofer." He didn't know where I was. I had to get the little guy. I reached out to him, but my head was a mess and he was too far away. Tyr, he'd be able to help.

"Tyr," I called, knowing a being such as him would be easy to connect with. Nothing. "Tyr? This is urgent, you better not be sleeping."

"Tyr is here."

"Show Woofer the way. Show him where I am, but both of you stay hidden. Understand?"

"Yes."

Damn, what was with him? Grumpy or what? That was my job. I'd had loads more practice.

I adjusted my pack, worried I'd flattened the dormouse, so checked quickly. She was still curled up, sleeping soundly, as cute as cute can be. I smiled despite the seriousness of the situation. Maybe she could help? Did I want to disturb a faery and have the ensuing grief? No, I did not. I stowed her away, then ensured I had my knife and gun handy. Pack secure, it was time to finish this.

I ran to the weather-worn door of the otherwise smart vicarage and pushed it open carefully. Inside was gloomy. It smelled stuffy, like someone had lived here comfortably for years. With senses on full alert, I crept along the hall, past a living room rammed with old furniture, glanced into a dining room with a large Victorian table polished until it shone, and then on into the rustic kitchen.

The sorcerer stood over the vicar, who was on his knees, gasping, eyes bugging, hands at his throat.

"No! Stop!" I shouted.

It was too late. The vicar keeled over and his head cracked on brown tiles.

"Now we begin," cackled the murderer.

"You killed a vicar! Why?"

"Because I needed him. He was my backup plan. I saw it. This is how it unfolds. His world is mine now. I will destroy you with his power, his innocence. You cannot win. Would you dare fight this man?"

"What? No, of course not. He's a bloody vicar. I'm not going to hurt an innocent."

"He was an innocent. A true believer. A kind man, and most generous. Now he's mine."

It suddenly dawned on me. "Fuck!"

This bloody annoying man cackled like all deranged magic-users do. "Oh yes, now you understand."

The vicar's body twitched. A pale pink liquid spurted from his mouth onto the tiles, then his head lifted and dead eyes snapped open. As the Necromancer stepped back and closed his own eyes, now seeing through those of the murdered clergyman, I questioned everything. What kind of world allowed such things to happen? Such people to exist?

And then I remembered. That was why I was here. No doubt about it. I'd been sent to stop this monster. What other blasphemous things had he done? What other faiths had he desecrated? How many lives had he destroyed just to practice his dark arts?

I would never know, but I swore I'd kill him even as I ran out of the front door away from a dead man of the cloth now taken over by a twat in a tracksuit and expensive trainers. He could have at least worn a cloak and had a staff so I'd have known what I was dealing with. Mawr had it right; you knew what you were getting with Mawr. There ought to be a rule or something. Nametags at the very least. "Hi. I'm a twat, and a Necromancer."

The rain had returned with a vengeance. It blasted me as I dashed across the already flooded lawn. I skidded as I tried to turn, and slid along the ground, soaking the seat of my jeans, but was up and away as fast as you'd expect when chased by a dead vicar with an evil grin on his face, brandishing an impressive Japanese kitchen knife.

The sky was bleak, the temperature more akin to winter, and I wondered if Tyr had taken cover. I got to the gate but it was jammed, or I was too panicked to figure out the latch, so I hopped over the wall and got some distance.

When I turned, the vicar was lodged against the stonework, in all kinds of trouble. It was because the sorcerer was still inside the house. Now was my chance.

From what I knew of this dark art, it meant that while he was directing the body, he wasn't using his own. He'd have to release his hold on it if he wanted to be able to see through his own eyes. Basically, he took over a corpse, but lost his own sight and mobility. But there were exceptions, I was sure of it, so didn't want to do anything too foolish. Nevertheless, as the vicar tried to climb over the wall, so I sprinted to the side and out of his sight, then hopped back into the garden and pelted into the house, knife out, ready to end this.

As I entered the kitchen, the necromancer was stirring. His eyes opened lazily, but widened in shock as I ran at him as hard as I could. His arm went up and he managed to shift position enough for the blade to stab right through his hand rather than his heart. I used my momentum to swing his arm out as I spun around and jammed the hilt against the wall. He screamed, but I was just getting started, and tugged hard to release the knife whilst rotating to provide extra force, which I used to smack the back of my head into his face. He grunted, bone crunched, and I figured I was almost done.

But he wasn't finished yet, far from it. Whispers insinuated themselves into my being, powerful because of the proximity. I was rooted to the spot and it would have been the end of me if it wasn't for a voice closing in by the second.

"Soph play ball with Woofer?"

"If you come and save me, then sure," I told my absolute bestest buddy, especially now Tyr was being a grumpy teenager.

I got a mental image of a very determined dog, but he was still several miles away. He vanished from my mind for a moment, and then I felt a sense of release as Woofer tore at the blasphemous magician's leg.

He roared with rage as he tried to shake Woofer free. I spat blood and punched out hard with the knife, but my movements were sluggish, and although I got him in the armpit above the vest, I doubted it was fatal.

Tyr screamed into the building, wings tucked in yet still hardly fitting through the hallway with all its furniture, then pounded into the mark and sent him flying across the kitchen.

Tyr shook himself out and turned his head to stare at the man as he panicked and tried to run. Tyr blocked his path. I dove at the Necromancer and palm-slammed his head against the wall, with every intention of it coming out the other side. In lovely little splintered bits.

As his head rebounded, and with impressive determination, the Necrobastard popped me on the nose—definitely broken, kicked Woofer—definitely a cracked rib, then shot Tyr—definitely pissed off.

The bullet dropped to the floor in front of Tyr. It hadn't even dented his thick skull. The dragon focused his gaze on the shooter.

"No fire," I warned Tyr.

"Tyr needs this," he whispered.

"No fire. No feeding."

Tyr turned his head on thick neck muscles—he'd definitely grown even larger since I last saw him—and stared deep into my eyes, his sclera almost black, so deep was the lust and craving. A true addiction, I now accepted. I understood my friend's desire. I became something else when in that zone, but my words must have got through as rather than belch flame, Tyr lunged forward with incredible speed and vomited acid onto the guy as I backed away. Maybe Tyr held back because he remembered my words. That if he disobeyed, he would not be part of this family. He loved Jen so much, loved all of us, but her especially.

It was just a shame Tyr puked on his prey's already punctured hand. The acid ate through the flesh and bone, but it was a badly placed puke by Tyr and most hit the floor. Tiles sizzled, Woofer crawled away whimpering, and as I dodged the spreading pool, the bastard ran out of the house. I jumped the acid and followed closely behind, whilst holding a mental conversation with the animals.

"Stay inside. Do not come unless I call," I warned Woofer and Tyr. "You okay, Woofer?"

"Chest hurt."

"I know. Stay still. It's probably a busted rib. We'll talk about how you got here so fast later. Tyr, good job. No fire," I added.

"Tyr want blood."

Hell, he better do as I told him, I thought, as I chased after this man who had become a bloody annoyance. I shut the door behind me and called again for Tyr to remain inside. We couldn't have a bloody dragon flying around a churchyard, breathing fire and killing mourners or worshippers. That was all kinds of wrong.

Drones buzzed overhead even through the rain. They amassed like this was a mighty fine spectacle. I gave them the finger, and sprinted after the now-wounded dabbler in all that gives magic a bad name, through a downpour so violent visibility became almost non-existent in the space of several seconds.

Something grabbed me by the ankle and I face-planted onto the flooded lawn. I got a mouthful of grass, soil, and filthy water, but pushed up instantly onto my knees. I stared into the bloodshot, faraway eyes of the vicar. He snarled, then tore at my face with splintered nails as he snapped at me with chattering jaws. One of his teeth had somehow got smashed.

"Sorry, vicar, but you're already dead." I punched him reluctantly in the face and shoved him away, feeling undeniably dirty, immoral, and convinced I'd secured my place in Hell. When up until now it had only been good odds, but not stamped "No chance of reprieve."

This was wrong on so many levels, and I was not a religious man.

Where was this bloody fool? I'd destroy him.

I ran away from the squirming vicar. This was getting too much; I needed to find the Necro and finish him off. I vaulted the wall, sped into the cemetery, and searched for him, but vision was poor and there was blood in my eyes. I ran around the outside of the church to no avail, so cautiously opened the door and peered inside. It was cool, and beautiful. Serene, and uncontaminated by the likes of me. He wasn't in here.

I turned away, moved back into the cemetery. Fresh flowers and headstones glistened in the rain even as it grew darker. Roiling clouds amassed overhead as the wind tore at my hair. The drones were gone.

The vicar charged me, hate in his eyes, his ruined face twisted in a cruel snarl. As I stepped aside, I slipped low and tripped him as he tried to slow. We rolled in the mud, punching and batting each other, but I couldn't bring myself to stab him, knowing it would make no difference as he was already dead.

He was frenzied, directed by the Necromancer, wherever the bastard was. I had to stop this. I had to act.

Ah, the eyes. I punched out so his head snapped back, then did what I had to do with the utmost regret. I stabbed both his eyes quickly, pop, pop, then rolled off, gasping, and crawled away. It took several attempts, but I finally got to my feet and stood there, getting my breath back as he fumbled about in the dark.

Dark?

Night had fallen with a heavy load of blood-soaked misery as I stood there, fucking done for. But what the hell? It wasn't evening, was it?

I'd had breakfast then messed around with this guy. It must just be lunch time. It was him, screwing with things, taking time and feeding on it. But no, said my addled brain, that wasn't a thing. Maybe that's why I'd got funny looks from the cafe owner and they seemed like they were shutting up shop. That was dinner, not breakfast. It truly was night. Was I losing my mind? Why hadn't I checked the time?

The vicar stumbled about, arms outstretched like a zombie, but then he simply went limp and fell to the ground. The Necromancer had finished with him, hopefully for good this time.

"Come out, come out, wherever you are," I sang to myself, as I wandered between ancient headstones and those just erected. I paused at the sound of a muffled groan, spun three-sixty to find the source, but saw nothing. The rain stopped as suddenly as it had begun. I listened again. There it was. What was it? My gaze lifted and out from the ground of an old grave clawed a truly macabre sight. Nothing but bones and flaps of skin. Caked in mud, and with long fingernails and wispy strands of hair plastered to its skull.

The corpse teetered, then fell, but somehow regained its footing and came stumbling after me. Something unholy, impossible, not real. This guy was powerful, but this was purely for show. As more of them came from ancient graves where the wooden caskets had rotted and he could force them to claw their way out, I merely moved away. They had no strength, no power, no way to defeat me.

Distracted by such a blasphemous sight, he crashed into me and sent me flying. I cracked my head on a large statue of an angel and almost blacked out. But I wasn't beat yet. I morphed, came right up behind him, and delivered my death blow. But he was fast too, and vanished only to reappear on my left. He tore open my side with his blade as he slid it in then sliced right even as I turned and thrust my own knife deep into his good arm. The other was nothing but a seething stump of pink flesh, but he had serious stamina, I'll give him that. But nothing else.

He hissed, used my own weight against me as he grabbed my shirt then dragged me over so I was face-down in the dirt. As the returning rain splashed muddy water into my eyes, and I fumbled to find my knife, he kicked me brutally in the head. I must have blacked out for a moment, because when I came to I saw the second kick coming and rolled aside. Good job it was trendy footwear, not work boots, or I would have been done. As it was, I was close to exhaustion, and he cackled as his eyes rolled up and the inanimate corpses of those long put to rest crawled forward and raked at my clothes and skin once more.

With an animalistic scream, I shucked them off and tore at a femur until it came loose. Slipping and sliding, I rose as fast as I could and hammered the makeshift weapon into the Necromancer's head. The brittle bone splintered and he sneered as I stepped away, readying myself for my next move. The re-animated dead fell to bits as he glared at me, his focus unwavering even though he was broken and bleeding badly.

"Just die," he hissed, as his whispers reached a new level of intensity.

I could do nothing but run to put considerable distance between me and his magic.

I tripped, and careened headfirst into a gravestone.

Unholy Union

No, no, no. This was beyond. Too much.

On all fours, I focused on the gravestone, unable to tear my eyes away even as the ground beneath me writhed and bucked. Even if he was behind me and ready to strike, I would have neither known nor cared, because this was more than I could cope with. More than my sanity could bear.

I read the epitaph.

Here Lies Nathan Blaine

Beloved Son of Soph and Rebekah

1882-1891

We Miss You So Much

My boy, my sweet, innocent boy. Dead for a hundred and forty-three years now. I screamed into the night as I recalled the year I turned two-hundred and one. One of the worst years of my long, often cruel existence. Would this madness never end? Maybe it would. I should let it. I should just lie down and let my poor, sweet child take me. Maybe then we'd both rest in peace.

This was unholy, too cruel. But maybe I deserved it. Maybe this was my reward for the atrocities I'd committed.

The fight was gone from me. There was nothing left. For so long I had raged against the world, did what it took to survive. Killed those who stood in my way. But this? It brought home that I was not the man I had believed. I had done terrible things. But worse, I had let terrible things happen. My boy, my little boy, one of many children lost over the years, but this had been different. This was my fault.

Memories of four years ago surfaced, when I sat on the Great Orme, staring down at the pier mixed with memories of much longer ago. Why had I returned there? Was this because of that? Did they know? Did the Necromancer know? Was that it? He knew. He read me, saw into me, and chose this as his most potent weapon. Love.

Clever, but beyond barbaric. Was there no honor left in this world? None at all? I laughed madly. There was no honor, and I was fooling myself if I believed I had any. I killed people to save my own skin. Even let my boy die. All the things I was capable of, yet I could not save him. Now he would rise from the grave to drag me down, but nowhere near as deep as he had sunk that day.

My beautiful wife and our two adorable children. A different time, a different me.

We were at the beach, laughing and playing in the sand, and the children wanted to swim. We suggested the pier first, then a splash in the water. The children were beyond excited, as this was their first trip of such magnitude. It was no mean feat to travel from Liverpool to Llandudno with two small children by horse and cart. Roads weren't like they are now, and there were no ubermarkets.

We traveled for the longest time, arrived late in the day, and all of us were keen to get our brand new tent assembled and have a fire and cook sausages. Camping had just become all the rage, and we weren't alone on the newly commissioned site. Families laughed and joked all around us, with plenty of choice swearing from men wearing suit and tie and sporting flat caps, tasked with assembling their temporary homes.

We had the best evening ever. We played games, we burned our sausages, and the children fell asleep exhausted. I stayed up late talking with my just-as-exhausted wife; we were still so much in love.

Next day saw us exploring the beach. Then the fateful trip to the pier.

I can picture it clear as day. Running along the pier, holding hands and skipping. We got to the end, marveled at the vastness, laughed at the seagulls bickering. I lost my hat as a strong gust swept on by. Everyone giggled and said I looked funny without it.

My son, my young, darling pride and joy, with gifts only just emerging, bent over the rail to watch the hat as it sank, and then he fell. Just like that, he was gone. It was a truly surreal moment, when time slows, events seem dream-like, and reality bends as your mind recoils.

My wife shrieked, my daughter cried. I pulled off my boots and coat then jumped into the freezing water. It was dark and I could see little, but I dove down, searching frantically, my heart hammering, my lungs fit to burst, my mind reeling.

Over and over, I surfaced for air then dove under. Why wasn't he floating? He should have come up by now. I found him eventually. He was beginning to rise back up, and I grabbed an arm then gripped him under his chin, got him onto his back, and swam for the shore.

A group of men waded out to help me as my wife screamed and women took the children away from the beach. They dragged us both out and I lay there, panting, half-drowned on the pebble beach as I stared at the face of my dead son. He was blue; I remember that so well. His face was blue. His eyes were open. And he was dead.

We took him home to Liverpool, wrapped in hessian in the back of the cart, and then we laid him to rest in this graveyard. My wife left two days later; I never saw her or my daughter again. In the note she'd written, she said she didn't blame me, that it wasn't my fault, but she left me anyway. She took my lifeline, my darling girl, and vanished.

I never tried to find her; I gave her the freedom she needed. I understood. I was too much of a reminder. He took after me, had my mannerisms, even looked like me. Same hair, same eyes. She had to get away. But I was denied both my son and my daughter. It was as though they had all died that day. Why couldn't she have stayed?

Alone for so long then. Nothing but meaningless encounters and short relationships that fizzled out eventually, as I couldn't muster the energy needed to live a life with someone. To have children again, risk the hurt.

I ran on auto-pilot for years. Killed without remorse or even thinking. I took out my frustrations, my loneliness, in the only way open to me. Year after year, note after note, I became more brutal, more capable, and the jobs got harder as my prowess came on in leaps and bounds. There was no quarter given; there was no pity or mercy. My emptiness was all I knew, and I reveled in the death as it was the only time I felt alive. But I knew I was broken. Yet slowly, over the years and against all the odds, I settled into acceptance. Never forgiveness, but acceptance.

Of all the children, it had been the hardest. Maybe because I felt to blame, maybe because I had lost not one but two children and a wife. But mostly because I knew he would have lived such a long life. It was doubly cruel. We would have been friends, companions for life, and all that was stolen.

And now it was all over. Now I would finally be reunited with my boy.

I lay there, beaten. Finally beaten. Broken, more like.

The ground shifted and the headstone fell away from me. I wished it had come the other way, smashed my head in and put an end to this insanity. I lay on the soaked grass as the rain pelted me, and watched my son's marker fall in slow motion then thud to the earth. The stone was cheap; it cracked and split in three.

Soil erupted around me and deep cracks opened. From out of the darkness came whispers of longing, soul-crushing calls for warmth and comfort. A call for Father. I was pretty far gone by now, but I knew this wasn't a voice from the grave. This was the damn sorcerer and his twisted whispers insinuating their way into my mind.

I squirmed, my body shivering despite the humidity of the night. Sweat poured off my body but I was freezing, gripped in the icy hold of death itself. Weird green gasses and noxious fumes slithered and snaked from the fissures as the earth sank in. Then my dead son clawed his way out of his place of rest, one excruciating moment after another.

Somehow, I was sitting, knees up tight to my chest, my arms wrapped around my shins, as I sank down while he rose up. Tiny arms and then a foul, filthy head, all covered in scraps of rotten rag and strips of leathery skin, emerged from the holy earth as he dragged himself up and out of the rotten coffin. Empty eye sockets stared only at me. The skeleton was all that remained, that and the rags, so there was no way this pile of bones could remain connected without the whispers of the sorcerer.

And yet, from somewhere, I knew I had to act. I must not give up, must never give in. My pack was still buckled tight, and I fumbled with the catch then released it. I pulled out the matchbox and slid back the lid.

"Help me, Malka. Please help me. For god's sake, help me."

Rain fell on the dormouse's tiny body. Her whiskers twitched, then she curled up tighter and began to snore.

I laughed. I laughed like a madman. I didn't deserve to be saved. I had no right. There was no last-minute reprieve, life didn't work like that, so I closed the lid and put her back in my pack as my son's bones wrapped around my legs.

"And now your fate is sealed," said the one who would finally defeat me. He spoke almost sadly as he stood over me, his body a wreck, blood washing from his broken face. "I have changed the future, Necrosoph, and you shall be no part of it. I see it now. All is change. All is chaos. This world will implode, you will have no part to play. I will flourish and the Necroverse remains as it was. The notes endure," he shrieked, raising his face to the dark sky.

"You want the notes to endure?" I gasped. "I came to kill you because of them."

"As it should be. I am part of the game, this is right. I will endure like the notes. I have been tested and found capable. Your timeline is gone; all is change. Your lineage will falter now. What was to be is no more. Don't you understand? This is more than you, Soph. This is about the future. Your daughter, her children, the future of the Necroverse. Ah, I see it so clearly. It is beautiful." He spread his arms wide and tilted his head back once more. His eyes closed and he smiled, lost to a vision only he could see.

"No," I croaked, as my son gripped my shirt and clawed his way upwards to my face.

The fool's eyes snapped open and he spat, "No!? You dare question my abilities?"

"Yeah, you fucker, because I bet you never saw this coming. Unicorns aren't part of your pathetic seer abilities. He's properly magic. Pure, innocent, and a good bloody aim." I spat dirt.

The sorcerer's body convulsed and he was lifted high in the air as five feet of sparkling, pure horn burst through his chest.

Bernard shook his head, the sorcerer weightless like a rag doll, then he thrust his horn forward and down and the dead Necro thumped to the ground at my feet.

The bones on my body went limp. Disconnected limbs rolled off but the skull rested on my knees against my chest. Black sockets stared at me, accusing.

I asked for forgiveness. I don't know if I received it.

Gasping, sick as a dog, and close to insane, I wriggled free of my son's bones and scrabbled away on hands and knees. I spied my knife and clutched it like a lifeline, then grabbed the sorcerer's head and whispered, "Nobody threatens my little girl. You can't see shit. You know nothing." I don't know how many times I thrust the knife into his neck and face, but it was a lot. Finally, all energy spent, I let his head go and clambered unsteadily to my feet, using Bernard as support.

"Thank you," I told Bernard. "You saved me. You saved us all, I think."

Bernard hung his head and stared at the corpse. "I killed him. I never kill. I'm not supposed to."

"I know. I'm sorry, and I shouldn't have asked. I wouldn't have, but he spoke of Jen, that my death would change things, that she wouldn't be what she is meant to be. I had to survive. I'm sorry."

"It's okay," he said brightly, seemingly over it. "Shall we go?"

"Not yet. I have a few things to do. And I'm not sure I can move much."

As I did move, and pain erupted all over my body, so I felt the presences behind me. Two people. I spun, ready to give all I had left, but the knife dropped from my hands and I hung my head, shamed and beaten.

"You shouldn't have come. You shouldn't see this. Best you leave."

"Why do you think we moved back to Liverpool?" said my long-lost wife with sympathy. "I'm sorry, Soph, I made a terrible mistake. It wasn't your fault, it was mine. Not Nathan, but what happened afterwards. I should never have taken our daughter from you. Soph, meet your daughter. Adina, meet your father. I am so sorry, both of you."

Adina ran forward and wrapped her arms around me. She smelled of coffee and lemons. She gripped so tight I couldn't help but yelp. She moved to let go. "Don't," I told her. "Don't let go just yet."

"I won't," she promised.

After what felt like an eternity, I released her and she took a step back. I took two. "Look at me. Look at what I did. At our son. I ruined it all again."

"You did no such thing. You had to return; it was inevitable. You didn't do this, he did." She pointed at the dead sorcerer. "I know him, we all do. His time was due. I'm amazed it took so long. But why you?"

"Because they like playing their games. Look at our son, your brother. This is insane."

She took it in her stride, as though it was the norm. Many years had passed, and maybe she'd done her mourning, maybe not. But there was no denying that seeing your child's bones like this should snap something inside.

"Why isn't this breaking you?"

"He's dead, Soph. A long time ago. I have forgiven myself. All that remains is your forgiveness."

I slumped to the ground, unable to cope. "My forgiveness? I never blamed you for a thing."

"I know, and that's the worst part of all. I left you when you needed me the most. I took her away from you. Took them both. Ruined our love. I left you alone."

"I deserved it."

"No, you didn't. You deserved to have your family around you, but I couldn't cope, couldn't bear seeing him in you. Everything you said or did. So I ran like a coward and took Adina with me. But we came back decades ago. I never tried to contact you, knew it was too late for that, but we heard you were back, news travels fast around here, and we figured it might end here."

"Why? How did you know?"

"We have our ways," said Adina. "We listened for the whispers, and we waited. We heard it begin and came when we could. Is that really my brother?" Adina walked over to the pile of bones beside the broken headstone. "We haven't been for so long. It feels like another life. So many years ago. Goodbye, brother, I wish I had known you." My daughter bent and touched the skull, then stood and turned back to me. "Let's put the past behind us."

"Let's bury our son together, as is right," agreed her mother.

"Bloody unicorns," I muttered, turning to give Bernard the daggers. He returned my gaze with unflinching, knowing eyes. He planned this. He knew word would reach them, that maybe they would even help. Sometimes he was beyond wise, always he was beyond annoying. "Thank you, my friend." Bernard nodded his head then turned away and wiped his horn in the grass.

"Do you forgive me," asked Rebekah.

"What? Of course. There is nothing to forgive."

"There is, Soph, so much. How could I have ever left you? You are such a good man. I wronged you in the worst possible way. I took it all from you. You missed our beautiful daughter growing up, seeing what she became. Now she is older, and wise, and I denied you both so much. I'm sorry. Please forgive me, both of you."

"Mother, I have already told you. I understand, and I forgive you."

"I forgive you," I croaked, the words not sounding right at all.

And yet, by merely saying these words, I found my own forgiveness, my own peace. I had finally confronted the past. Now all that remained was to bury it. For good this time.

After freeing the grumbling animals from the vicarage, and rather awkward introductions followed by a long rest, we spent the remainder of the night burying the risen corpses. My son was first. Our son. Adina's brother. Nathan was at peace once more. But some things can never be put to rest, and I found no solace in this task, only bile and vitriol. The others spoke of it being closure, but I felt none of that. Just anger and a deep sadness. All that had been lost, all that could have been, taken away from me once, then desecrated, too many memories resurfacing.

I was utterly beat. Filthy, exhausted, head a mess, body broken in numerous places. I wasn't sure how I'd managed to help bury the corpses, could remember little of it, but Bernard told me he helped. That often I stood there, numb, while he scraped away with his horn and hooves, and Rebekah and Adina used a shovel they retrieved, putting the dead back where they belonged.

I believed him.

Early morning, and the sun came out as if to mock me. Steam rose from the graveyard as the rain evaporated. My daughter stripped off my soaked, filthy clothes and gasped at the state I was in. They tended me gently, whispered their words over my broken body, but this damage needed more than they could give, although it helped numb the worst of it.

We all stood around as Tyr did as instructed. He purged over the sorcerer, using all his reserves to spew acid up and down his body. We watched him dissolve as the day broke over the church tower in a small cemetery in Liverpool. Far from home, far from family that knew and understood me, at least in part. I had my other family with me too, and the past, well, maybe it would remain buried this time.

And yet I knew it wouldn't, that it could never be forgotten. For I, like so many other Necros, was an aberration, and we must pay for the long lives we lead and things we do.

When all that remained was a patch of sizzling earth, we walked away from that place. I would never return.

At the entrance to the cemetery, I asked an important question to the two women standing before me.

"Have the years been good to you? Are you happy? Do you have husbands and children and nice lives?"

"We do. We have many children and many grandchildren, and on it goes," said Rebekah. "Our lives are good. But I've missed you, Soph, and I never forgot you. I didn't speak of you for many years to Adina, and I regret it deeply. But time heals wounds, at least in part, and I moved on. What else can we do? But we came back, and we wanted to. Something made us return long ago, and we have our lives here now. You can be a part of that, if you wish?"

"No, I'm sorry, but I can't. We're strangers, much as it hurts to say it. You live your lives. You want no part in mine. Trouble is coming. I'll hurt you again. Best to leave and never look back."

They understood. Both knew this would be the answer. Rebekah knew me too well, understood me maybe more than I understood myself, even though we were together for but a brief moment in our lives.

It pained me deeply to say these things, but they really were better off without me. But mostly it was for selfish reasons. I couldn't be a father to this grown woman. Couldn't be a friend to my wife who had left me in my darkest moment. I loved her, yet hated her for what she had done. And although I gladly offered forgiveness I never suspected she sought, part of me could never truly forgive her for leaving me. Even though I felt it was my fault, and now understood maybe I wasn't to blame, I could not be a part of their lives.

I had a future far away, with a family that I loved and cherished beyond all else, and I would not put that at risk. I vowed never to involve them with my previous life in this way because, when I thought about it, I simply didn't have it in me. That wouldn't be fair on any of us.

So we said our goodbyes. I wished them well, and they left.

They didn't look back.

Homeward Bound

The city was beautiful in the early morning. I turned to my dog and asked, "So, how did you manage to cross the city and arrive miles away so fast?"

"Woofer copied Soph."

"I think you better explain."

"Can't. Saw Soph become little bits, you travel far that way. Soph called for Woofer, so copied you. Hurts so bad. Not like it. Play ball?" His tail wagged hopefully.

"Um, not right now. Sorry. So you morphed? But you can't do that," I told him.

"Oh? Woofer thought he could."

I couldn't argue with that, and I didn't have the mental energy to figure that one out at the moment. It wasn't like it was the weirdest thing that had happened to me recently.

It was time to go.

Woofer trotted along beside Bernard as he weaved his way through the city streets. Tyr flew high, well above the drones and the skyscrapers.

I held on to Bernard, slumped forward, resting against his warm, pure body, heedless of the pain, my ravaged body as nothing compared to my damaged mind.

The sorcerer had been powerful, right up there with the best, and yet we were victorious. How was that? By rights, I should have been dead. He was way above my non-existent pay grade, yet once again I had emerged the victor. Not that it was down to me. Bernard had saved the day. Poor guy, I shouldn't have asked that of him. It wasn't his place, not in his nature, and the last thing I wanted to do was corrupt him.

"Are you okay, Bernard?" I asked, as he trotted past Radio City Tower, hardly a soul in sight, the streets crisp and clean thanks to several industrious road sweepers.

"I think so. I have killed before, you know. Don't you remember?"

"I remember. And I know you have a past you have never told me about. But this was different, wasn't it?"

"Yes, I suppose. I'm a unicorn though, and we are unlike other creatures. If it felt wrong, I would have been unable to do it. It felt right. Not good. Just right."

"You saved us. You saved me, anyway. Thank you, my friend."

He didn't reply.

We crossed the bridge. Yesterday's crowd had dispersed. In its place a lone police car with two men inside, probably with the air-con running. They sipped coffee out of a flask. I waved as we passed. They nodded, then paid us no heed.

The long road home lay before us, but we would be there in an hour or two once Bernard got up to speed.

I felt nervous, as though my family would see what had happened, could read the changes in me. Recoil at seeing my twisted mind. The killings. The endless killings.

And yet I understood they would love me anyway. For this was our lot. Necro. Slowly, as Bernard took us away from the city, I began to find a little peace. The torturous, aching journey of healing had begun. Was this really closure for this ancient episode of my past life? Had I finally put the demons to rest? Had I forgiven myself for not saving my son when I was capable of so much? I could kill, why not save? Was that it? Why I had never sought forgiveness for not saving him? The sheer injustice of it all?

And yet there was more to consider here. The sorcerer's words. Not merely a wizard, not just a man who studied magic, learned the whispers, delved into other realms, he was a true sorcerer. Able to meddle in the future, see what lies before us. He had known, or at least thought he knew, what would become of us. And he hadn't wanted it.

What was he trying to destroy? And why? He had been marked; they wanted him dead. Because he would otherwise seek us out? Or because they knew he was the only one to stop us from fulfilling our future?

So many questions. No answers. But I was slowly learning more. Although I couldn't untangle the web of truths and half-truths, hints and revelations, I knew one thing for certain. I was becoming dangerous to myself, to my family, to the very fabric of our being. I wasn't dumb enough to believe I could change things, save us from this game we played, but it was now clear something wasn't quite right.

The elf on the boat. The way Jukel had been disposed of. The eye in the sky and the notes swirling. Now the words of the sorcerer. They all meant something. But there would be no big reveal, me saving the world. I wasn't that naïve, had become way too jaded to believe that. But over time, I was convinced I would garner knowledge, dangerous truths, and if that helped my daughter mature and fulfill her destiny, then I could live with that.

Or try to.

Bernard warned he was ready to get us home. I hauled Woofer onto my lap, and soon we were enveloped in sparkles of joy. Floating on fluffy clouds, tickling the air full of rainbows, and dreaming sweet dreams of playful puppies and licking ice creams in the back garden.

It was a long way home, but at least we were going there.

Home. I did have a home. Somewhere I belonged.

I smiled before I lost consciousness and didn't come to until I fell off Bernard outside the gate to the one place in the world I felt I truly belonged.

Woofer landed on my chest, and a solid Lab on a broken body after falling off a unicorn is no fun at all. I groaned, but didn't bother to move, as I just wasn't up to it. Woofer licked my face and I laughed. What else could I do?

"Soph want to play ball?" he asked, then limped off. He was back a moment later, red ball in his mouth, tail wagging, eyes eager. "Play ball now?"

"Um, maybe later," I gasped, now sure several ribs were broken. "But Woofer, you aren't well. Don't forget about your wound. Look at your side. And your leg's hurt, remember?"

Woofer thought for a moment, then he looked at the raw wound on his side. He dropped the ball, his eyes rolled up, and he keeled over onto my chest again.

I screamed. Yep, broken for sure.

Woofer remained out of it. Poor guy. It was home and sausages for him from now on. He'd earned his stripes. Now it was time for him to retire. I doubted I'd get any objections. Especially about the sausages.

I lay there for a while, smiling through the hurt, with my dog on my chest and my unicorn asking if he could open the gate.

"You can try," I wheezed, then blacked out.

When consciousness returned, it was with sheer panic. I clawed at the ground, believing I was buried alive. The weight of the earth heavy on my chest. It was just my comatose dog. I struggled for breath, but it was likely my lungs had collapsed, and panic set in again. Was it just Woofer, or had I punctured a lung?

I rose onto raw elbows and somehow managed to get Woofer off me. His nose twitched and slowly his eyes opened.

"Woofer feel funny."

"I know. Just stay there. We'll get you fixed up."

"I can't open the gate," complained Bernard. "How does it work?"

"Tyr will burn to a crisp. Get everyone inside. Call for help."

"Don't burn the bloody gate," I insisted. "Bernard, just press the doorbell with your horn or hoof or something. Tyr, go find Phage." I collapsed back onto the ground. I couldn't feel my legs, and I was now certain I had a punctured kidney. My side throbbed madly. It was hot and I was soaked in sweat. Infection had set in.

There was a crunch. I guess Bernard hadn't managed to navigate the complexities of a doorbell. I turned my head to see his horn stuck in the gate, the plastic remains of the doorbell scattered across the gravel. Unable to help it, I laughed. It hurt so bad, unbelievably bad, and I laughed at that too.

From my prone position, face turned towards the house, I saw Phage running towards me.

Saved at last.

Darkness enveloped me once more.

I expected to wake up screaming, but instead I woke to find the pain was mostly gone, but I was unable to move my limbs. My head turned and I was looking into the eyes of my wife. What a sight she was! My spirits lifted immediately.

"Hello, handsome." Phage smiled and all was right with the world.

"Hello, beautiful lady. Um, I can't move."

"I whispered for you. You're in a bad way, but you'll live. You need to go to the hospital, and you'll be there for a while, but I wanted a moment first."

"Where are we?"

"Why don't you take a look?" Her eyes twinkled with mirth, but there was concern and sadness too.

I looked, and realized I was exactly where I'd fallen. "Oh, I'm here."

"You sure are. With me." Phage was lying right beside me, body warm against mine. "You made it. Another year."

"Just. Um, is this a dream? It feels all floaty."

"Not a dream. It's the whispers, carrying away the hurt on the breeze. I wish I could heal you myself, but doctors will do a much better job. But let's not talk of such things now. Let's just look at the sky. You and me. How does that sound?"

I turned back to my wife and smiled. "That sounds like a fine idea. There is nowhere in this world I would rather be right now. Nobody else I would rather be with. Not ever."

Phage smiled at me again.

We lay there, outside our front gate, and stared up at the infinite blue sky. There wasn't a cloud to be seen. Just pure, deep blue. Full of infinite possibilities. I have no idea how long we lay there like that, minutes or hours, but I felt at peace.

I felt loved. I truly felt like I belonged.

When I awoke, it was in the hospital.

Machines beeped.

I had a catheter.

My world smelled of disinfectant and rotten fruit.

A Daughter's Concern

"What do you do?"

"Huh?" I asked, feeling groggy from the meds I was still on even after weeks in the hospital.

Jen shifted awkwardly on the edge of the bed in the private room that felt more like a prison than a place to get fixed.

"What do you do? You and Mum? You go off every year and usually come back hurt. I've been trying to remember when I was little, and as far back as I can recall, you get hurt. So, what do you do?"

"I suppose I'm just unlucky. Every time I go away on business, I seem to get attacked. Haha, maybe I should stay at home."

Jen reddened and did her angry face. I wanted to cuddle her and tell her everything would be alright, that there was nothing to worry about. That Daddy was fine, would always be there for her. But it wasn't Daddy anymore, it was Dad, and she was eleven and far from stupid.

"Come on! You go off with Tyr. This time you even took Woofer and Bernard. What's the deal? And Tyr's bloody massive now. And Woofer keeps vanishing. I found him on the roof the other day."

"Jen! That's the first time you've sworn in your life." I was shocked. "And he's still morphing, is he? Damn, we need to figure out what's going on there." Apparently, he'd been at it for over a week now. Phage didn't know what to do. Neither did I.

"Is it? You reckon? The first time? And stop changing the subject. Anyway, I've heard things. From other Necros."

"Where did you hear that term?"

"Dad, I don't live under a rock. People talk. You and Mum talk. I've heard you say the word and I know what it means. We see Grandma every year now, and I know that never used to happen. You think I don't hear you all talking? About notes? What are notes? And about other stuff. I want to know."

I eased myself up the bed to get comfortable, or as comfortable as I could currently be, and I looked into the still mostly innocent eyes of my perfect daughter. A daughter I swore I would never leave, never let go of. "It's complicated, and I don't think you are ready to know everything yet, as you are still very young. But you know we all have gifts, right?"

"Of course. Zoolinguism, that's what it's called, right? Talking to animals."

"Yes, but that's just one of your gifts. One of mine. Your mother can't do it, but she can do other things. Same as Grandma can. Same as me."

"Like what?" Jen bit her lip, her default move when worried or nervous.

"I can't tell you yet. You're too young. Soon, I promise I will tell you soon. When I get out, me, you, and your mum will sit down and talk this whole thing through. But yes, you are what is known as a Necro. Your life will be very different to the other people you know. Same as mine is, and your mother's. We're different."

"All this magic and stuff? Dragons and unicorns and immortal cats and talking animals? That kind of thing, you mean?"

"Yes, and dwarves in the basement. Other things too. Haha, sounds crazy, right?"

"I guess." Jen shrugged. This was her life. What she'd grown up with. "Like shifters? Like Stripe, the goblin? Can you do that? Wow, that would be so cool. Will I?"

"Jen, hold it." Damn, this was getting messy, and I knew I wasn't focused enough to think this through properly, decide what she should know. Phage and I had to do this together, talk it over first. "Each Necro has their own unique set of gifts, if you want to call them that. You're too young to have yours yet, and hopefully it will stay that way for a long time. Just like Tyr, you are supposed to develop slowly. Let your body and mind grow along with your ability. But you know you are different, don't you?"

"Course I do. I don't know why, exactly, but I can feel something inside, like I'm ready to burst. Like a supercool and amazing thing will happen soon and I'll be very different."

"Well, I was hoping those feelings were years away, as you're still very young, but we'll have to see. Just know your mother and I are here to help you, to guide you, and you must promise never to try anything unless you tell us first. Do you promise?"

"Try what?"

"Anything that isn't what your friends can do. I don't mean regular growing up stuff. I mean things your friends never talk about. Maybe flying, or turning into a rabbit." Jen's eyes went wide. "Whoa, I was joking."

"But is it a gift? Can some people do that stuff?"

"Kind of. Yeah. Listen, this is very important. It can be dangerous, and you could hurt yourself very badly, even die. You must promise me never to try anything without discussing it with us first. Promise me, Jen."

"I promise. So, what can you do?" Jen was the picture of daughterly innocence, trying to get round her old dad. She knew I found it impossible to resist her cute act.

"Oh no you don't, young missy. Don't you try that one on me while I'm in this state. I'll be home soon, and then we'll talk. I've probably already said too much in my addled state. But in the meantime, strengthen your bond with Tyr and keep him under control."

"I am, every day. He told me some of what happened. Not all of it. He said he wasn't allowed. But some. He said he saved you, killed someone, and read a book about dragons that an old wizard showed you. And he's going to be immortal and bigger than a bus, although he didn't know what a bus was, and that he can vomit acid. Is that true?" Jen stared at me, eager for more gruesome details.

I groaned. I needed to have a word with Phage, so she'd tell Tyr to shut his trap, but it appeared that train had already left the station.

"Tyr likes to exaggerate. But he's grown a lot, right? And he's dangerous now, so you must keep the special bond you two have. A dragon without emotional ties is a very, and I can't overemphasize this, very dangerous thing. Are you locking him up between letting him out?"

"Yeah, but he isn't happy. He wants his freedom. It seems mean."

"I know it does, but it's for his own good while he grows into his new size and gets his head straight. Think of it like this. You don't let a young puppy out to just do as he pleases and go where he wants. You keep them confined to let them develop and grow as safely as possible. If he isn't with one of us, then it can be dangerous. Even letting him out with you is risky, but he needs his exercise."

"He's sleeping loads anyway," shrugged Jen.

"Good, that's good. When I'm out, things will be different, I promise. We'll tell you what we can, but it won't be everything. You're old enough to understand that there are some things only adults should know, right?"

"I guess. I worry about you and Mum though. Why do you keep getting hurt? What do you do?"

"I'm sorry you worry. I don't want that. Try not to. I'm tough as old boots. You can count on that."

"Is that how you got all the scars? From this thing you do?"

"We'll talk about it when I get home. Thanks for visiting me every day. You don't have to. I know you've got things to do. Friends to hang out with."

"I like it." Jen smiled, then sprang forward and hugged me tight.

It hurt so much, and I don't mean because my body was far from mended.

Home at Last

Escaping from dreams of bones, I woke with a smile. I sniffed, took in the scent of my wife, her essence. Perfume and soap, shampoo and sweat. It was beautiful. I sniffed again, unable to stop my smile from spreading. I smelled old rugs and worn carpets. Beeswax, and wooden furniture bought long ago from makers whose names had never been known. Would it be wrong to remain like this for the rest of my days? Sniffing and grinning, never opening my eyes? Probably, and I'd need a pee at some point.

"Time to get up," I told myself, as I reluctantly opened my eyes.

Getting out of my own lovely bed felt like a cosmic joke. I had never been so weak, thirsty, or hungry, and never craved slippers more than I did this morning. And I absolutely needed that pee.

Knowing I still had to take things easy, but that I was thankfully over the worst, I was cheered by the knowledge I'd be back to my old self soon enough. It hadn't felt like it, but I healed fast, and my muscles would bounce back once I began moving about and taking some exercise. I swore if I never saw another daytime TV show in my life, it would still be too soon. Hospitals are great and all, but there is a serious lack of things to do.

Drooling as I thought of my pub, my animals, especially my wife, I eased my legs over the side of the bed and tentatively tried to stand.

I used the edge of the mattress for support, but it wasn't as bad as I'd anticipated. My legs didn't feel too bad, and it wasn't like I hadn't moved at all during my extended stay in hospital. A man's gotta pee and take a shower now and then.

I steadied myself at the window and looked out onto a barren winter landscape. Trees were bare, dormant until spring. A thin dusting of pure snow blanketed the ground, and I wondered if I'd missed Christmas. I loved Christmas. The sky was clear and deep blue in that unique way you only get to marvel at in the winter months. I longed to get out there and revel in the cool air. How were the animals? Were they warm and well fed?

The troll in the garden was covered in snow; he looked like a deformed snowman. I wondered if he enjoyed this more suitable weather.

Job's weird construction poked above the copse of trees, a strange insectile confusion of jutting beams and bizarre angular protrusions. Was it finished? It didn't look like it, but what was it meant to be anyway?

Padding over to the mirror, I checked myself out, expecting the worst. A skeleton wrapped in saggy skin maybe, or just something plain ugly. All sunken cheeks and massive beard. The reality wasn't quite so bad. I'd lost a little weight, but not much. My muscles had shrunk somewhat, but the definition was still there, and everything worked as it should. At least, I hoped it did. There was one thing that hadn't been used in months.

My beard had been trimmed, but I'd shave that off back to stubble. My hair was much longer, which I liked, but my cheekbones were disturbingly angular and I had this haunted look in my eyes. It was all understandable, but I smiled, because I was home and you can't beat being home.

The wounds were still red and angry looking, but the surgeons had done a first-class job of fixing me up, so once again, I thanked the NHS. I prodded the worst scar at my side; I nearly screamed as icy pain shot right up into my head then did an evil jig. Damn, that was tender. Nothing a nice homecoming fry-up wouldn't help repair.

"Soph is awake!" shouted Woofer, as he bounded into the room and plonked himself down in front of me.

"He sure is. How you doing, buddy?" I asked, rubbing his head.

"Happy."

"Good. That's good. Thanks for looking after everything while I was in the hospital. I missed you." I stroked his ears in the special way he loved, then squatted on aching legs and gave my dog the biggest cuddle ever.

"Woofer looked after everything. Played ball with Jen. Helped Phage in the kitchen. Had great games with Mr. Wonderful. Lots of things."

"That's great, haha. I bet they loved that. Especially Mr. Wonderful."

"Yes, now Woofer happy. You been gone so long. Lots of days. Months?"

"Yes, months. But I'm back now. Awesome to see you." I hugged him again and sensed the love pouring from Woofer. He was a good boy. "You did great on the job, a real help. How were you after? Were you okay?"

"Woofer had to go to nasty vet and have stitches. Stay in cage. Big bandage around tummy." His ears flattened. "But then I was better and came home and got given chicken and rice and had lots of fuss and extra blankets. Woofer like chicken."

"I know you do. Good job. So, you really are okay? Were you scared?"

"Not scared of anything!"

"Well, I was scared. Especially for you."

"Maybe Woofer a little scared."

I tickled under his chin and said, "You are very brave. Right, I need to get clean. See you in a bit?"

Woofer wagged his tail then trotted off; positive vibes emanated from his slightly more rotund than usual body. Guess he wasn't the only one who'd been taking it easy these last few months. He deserved it. He did much better than I'd expected, but I vowed he would live the easy life from now on.

Feeling chipper, because hey, I was alive so could continue to moan loudly and proudly about stuff, I cleaned myself thoroughly in my first real shower for months. The water was hot, the suds a delight, the pressure intense. I felt like I was being flayed alive after the weak dribble I'd endured at the hospital. Teeth brushed, ablutions complete, I dressed carefully, feeling better by the minute, and even did a few push-ups to test my abilities.

I got to seven and had to stop. My muscles ached and my side sent spasms of pain up into my teeth, and I'm not even sure that's a thing.

Not to worry. I had my looks.

Being home truly was wondrous. The longer I was absent, the deeper my heart ached to experience the joy I knew awaited my return. And this had definitely been the longest I'd been away by far. Rooms felt larger, the air cleaner, the smell of polish intoxicating—a rare occasion, as Phage was about as interested in housework as me. And oh, how refreshing the water. From a tap! Such a miracle of modernity. It still rocked my world to be able to lift a lever and have fresh, pure water gush out freely. Not that it was free, mind you, but heck, it was worth the cost. I don't know why, but this transfixed me, and it wasn't like we didn't have taps at the hospital. Maybe my head was still rather fuzzy.

Phage had sorted out my pack from the trip, and left a few of my belongings in my section of the wardrobe. I pulled out the matchbox and wondered if she'd opened it. Probably not. Maybe she couldn't, unless I gave her permission. She would have sensed it had something special inside, though. Her gifts were way beyond mine.

I slid the lid aside and smiled at the twitching dormouse, still curled up and sleeping away who knew how many years. Shame she hadn't come to my rescue, but maybe that was for the best? I decided to make her a gift to

Phage. She loved this kind of thing. I eased the lid closed and slid Malka into my shirt pocket.

Whistling, I headed downstairs in my own house, and what a luxurious feeling it was. The stairs were an issue though. After months without using them, it seemed my legs had forgotten how to navigate such a complex obstacle. I figured it out in the end, but I was sweating by the time I reached the bottom step.

"Hey, Mr. Wonderful. How are you today?" I asked, as I passed the cat where he sat by the front door, looking evil and plotting something dastardly.

"Good to see you," he said, and he swaggered over and rubbed himself against my legs. "He's mine. I own him. I own this house. I own this land. I own this door. The stupid dog is mine. I own—"

"You know I can hear that, right?" I said.

"You can't. I was keeping my thoughts to myself."

"Yes, I can. You can keep your thoughts to yourself, but you weren't. You were sending them out like we were talking. Stop being so bloody smug."

"Whatever." Mr. Wonderful resumed glaring at the air, daring anything to mess with him. Come and have a go if you think you're hard enough. At least he was nice for a moment.

Whistling, I continued my journey down the hall towards the kitchen, where it was strangely quiet. Jen would have left for school as I slept in, but Phage should be around. She was probably outside. Maybe she'd made me a surprise fry-up? Ooh, that would be awesome. Buoyed by my rumbling stomach, I forged ahead.

I walked past the open door to the living room and stopped dead in my tracks. The TV was on, the volume low. My beautiful chair creaked as though there was someone sitting in it, but I saw nobody. Hackles up, I eased into the room, cursing under my breath because I didn't have my knife. A Necro should always have his weapon. That was my rule. I inched forward, then jumped in front of the chair only to find Shey Redgold with his feet up, smiling happily, eyes glued to the TV.

"Hey, I'm watchin' that," he growled, angling his head to see around me. He waved me away like I was a bug, but I glared at him.

"What the hell are you doing? You're in my chair."

"You weren't usin' it. An' I'm watchin' the TV. It's so great. Do you mind?" He craned his neck again and I was forgotten.

"Hey, hey." I snapped my fingers and slowly he turned his attention from the screen. His eyes looked huge with his glasses on, the TV reflected in the lenses.

"Ssh, this is important. It's a show all about these people who live on the same street. They get up to all sorts. Crazy humans."

"Neighbours. It's called Neighbours. It's Australian."

"Is it? That's what they're called? Oh."

"Yes, it's been running for like ever. Why are you here? Does Phage know? Where is she?"

"She knows. Look, haha, these guys are crazy. Is it always like this? Do you all keep gettin' married to each other and get up to all sorts?"

"Oh yes, we all live like that."

His eyes widened in wonder. "Amazing." He slid sideways, almost horizontal, and ignored me.

I didn't have the energy to smack him, so moved over to the mantelpiece and carefully laid Malka there. I'd show Phage later; she'd be over-the-moon to have her own faery. Glaring at Shey Redgold, I left him to it and continued my quest in search of wives and fry-ups. He didn't even ask how I was.

Phage wasn't in the kitchen, so I decided to stretch my legs properly outside. I could check on the animals. Bet they hadn't even noticed I'd gone. With my wellies on, which was a monumental achievement, and a coat and hat, which was a lesson in how to make every part of your body hurt like your wounds were fresh, I stepped out of the kitchen door and into the frosty, sleepy world of a very British winter. Woofer ran ahead and rolled around upside down in the snow, telling me how awesome it felt, and that I should join him.

How wonderful it was here. Last time I'd been able to walk, it was either in stifling heat or crazy rain. Now I could almost believe the world was normal. The thin layer of snow was hard. The sharp crunch as I moved across the grass a sound as beautiful as any symphony. Water in watering cans was frozen. The world felt fresh and new. I breathed deep. It hurt my chest but I didn't care. A robin watched from the fence.

"Hello. Nice day, isn't it?"

"Beautiful day," he agreed. "This is my patch. Behave!" he warned.

"Will do," I said, smiling. Robins were so territorial and loved a fight. I hadn't met this guy before; wonder what happened to the other fella?

I moved slowly, enjoying the crisp air, my breath in front of me as I exhaled. Down past the chickens with a hearty hello, through another gate, past the orchard, then to the zoo. I could smell them. It smelled of home. Of hard work, steaming piles of fresh manure, and happiness. The unmistakable aroma of security and love.

The zoo was exactly that, a collection of creatures both rare and common. Some were magical beings of the Necroverse, able to communicate with all other animals, with gifts too varied to list, whilst others were simply creatures I had rescued or had been brought to me. Others simply found their way here one way or another.

Some slept for years at a time, others hardly ever. What they all had in common was a home. Somewhere safe, secure, where they would always have food and comfort. There were large buildings repurposed from old cattle sheds that housed many of them. Inside were goats and several pigs, Stripe, who I found curled up under a pile of straw, snoring away, and other small creatures like mice, ferrets, stoats, shrews, and even several horses so tiny you could hold them in the palm of your hand. If you could find them.

But most were just regular breeds, although several hedgehogs had a tale or two to tell. Anything seen as unusual by guests was housed separately so children could visit one building and play with the animals without it causing mass hysteria, or the risk of being eaten. It worked well, most of the time.

More fearsome animals had more secure housing, and were given appropriate levels of care or left to themselves apart from when fed, but they were all happy. Anyone could leave if they wished, but most stayed for a while, got themselves fixed up, and then remained. We spoke as I passed from one to the next; they greeted me warmly. A surprising number asked where I had been, if I was mended, others had no understanding of such things and didn't notice the passing of time the way we do, so I didn't begrudge them that.

Some of the more unusual animals greeted me in ways strange to humans, natural to them. A nibble of the ear, a whisper into my mind, a shiver down the spine. All were welcome and received with thanks.

I exited one building to enter the next, and continued the rounds. Other animals, like the meerkats, lived mostly outdoors with just small houses for when needed. Bernard had his own stables with his family and I spent a little time there, checking on Kayin and her parents. Bernard and Betty were happy, but both were tired and had been for years. But he was doing well, and I thanked him again for the part he'd played in recent events and for getting me home safely. He said he'd sworn off the sweet stuff for good, although I didn't believe him for a moment.

Then I went to visit Tyr.

I entered the barn and locked it behind me. As I peered up into the gloom, two fierce eyes studied me.

"What, you not going to come and say hello?"

"You are a stranger. Tyr not like strangers in his lair," he hissed. He dove right at me and I might have done a little yelp, but then he veered off and alighted on the ground and cackled like a fool.

"Damn! You scared the life out of me."

"Tyr learned to tell jokes. You looked so funny."

"Yeah, well, haha, guess you got me. Wow, you've grown even bigger."

"Tyr a true dragon now. Mighty and strong. Jen plays with Tyr almost every day and we are best friends." He studied me intently, like he was waiting for something.

"What's on your mind, friend?"

"Did Soph miss Tyr?"

"Yes, I did. I've been cooped up for months, nothing to do, hardly anyone to talk to. I missed you loads."

"Tyr needs a new home. Too big to get in and out now, must wait for door to open. Need freedom."

"I understand. You have grown fast, and I guess you need your independence. Give me a while to sort something out, okay? I need to have a think about how to do it. So, you have to be let out? But you sleep a lot, right, as you're young and growing, so give me some time. I need to know you won't fly off and cause trouble. Can you promise me that?"

"Tyr will try to behave."

"That's not what I asked. I need to know if you can come and go as you used to, that you won't hurt anyone. You understand?"

"Tyr understands. Would never hurt human unless Soph says so."

"Good. Now listen carefully, as this is important. I want you to give me your word, to swear it. You know what that means, right? If you make a promise? It's binding for dragons; you cannot take it back. A dragon of your age cannot break a promise. We read that in the book. Bad things will happen if you do. Do you promise not to hurt a human or to kill one without either me, Jen, or Phage giving the order?"

"Tyr promises."

"Okay, then leave it with me. We'll figure something out. Get you a bigger place. Anything you'd like inside?"

Tyr cocked his head to the side and thought. Damn, he looked so mature, but I knew that was far from the reality.

"Tyr wants thick pole to perch on. Comfy bed, and lots of food. Fresh."

"I'll see what I can do."

He nodded his thanks. I was about to lock the door when I turned back and looked at the dragon in my care. Should I leave the door open? He used to have his freedom to come and go as he pleased, but he was so young he could do no harm. Soon, I would give him his freedom again soon.

"Sleep well, my friend. The world will be yours again. Tonight we will go out into the fields and you can fly as high as you like." I closed and locked the door.

"Now, where's my bloody wife?" I wandered back up to the house and spied her through the kitchen window. My spirits lifted even higher. This was turning out to be the perfect day.

"It's me, your awesome husband," I announced to Phage, who quickly spun away from me and wiped at her face. She looked like she was crying. Her slender shoulders sagged, her head hung low. "What's up? You look worse than I feel." I stepped forward, but she tensed up.

"I got my note."

"Oh, hell, is it your birthday today already? The ninth? Sorry, I had no idea what the day was, wasn't even sure about the month. Damn, December. Sorry."

"I didn't expect you to remember. Goddamn!" Phage banged the table with her fist.

"Hey, hey, come on, it will be alright." I wrapped my arms around her from behind, making sure not to peek at her tightly clutched note. "Wow, you're stiff as a board. You'll be back in no time. Promise."

"You can't promise that," she whispered. "But that's not why I'm so angry."

"Then what?" I spun her around and looked into her eyes. Tears streamed down her face, her cheeks were bright red, and her forehead was soaked with sweat.

"That bad, eh? Somewhere far away? What, no, you haven't checked where yet, have you? You haven't even opened it. What gives?"

"Soph, I'm so sorry. And you only got out of hospital yesterday. I am so sorry."

"It's fine. I can manage without you for a few days. Haha, I'm a big boy now. And anyway, Jen will look after her old dad. See, nothing to worry about."

"No, it isn't that. Soph, I truly am sorry." Tears fell, her body shook. She stood back from me, laid the note out on the scrubbed pine table, then smoothed it until it lay flat.

"Careful! I almost took a peek."

"You have to look."

"What?"

"I said, you have to look," sobbed Phage. "Read it, Soph. Look at the note."

My eyes moved slowly from her face to the damn note and my heart went cold.

I read the name. *Necrophage.*

And there beneath it, I read another. *Necrosoph.*

"It's for both of us." Phage grabbed me and cried into my shirt.

"Guess we need to find a sitter then," I said, trying to keep it together when all I wanted to do was scream.

THE END

Find out what happens when Soph and Phage team up in Dragon Nights. Due for release January 2022.

Sign up at alkline.co.uk to stay updated about new notes, because book 3 pushes our beloved Necros further than they ever believed possible.

The Usual Chat

Argh, I didn't see that coming! At least Soph and Phage working together will give us a chance to learn a little more about their past. And we'll get to witness what Phage is capable of. Knowing where she grew up, it's bound to be impressive.

But how will they work as a team? Who wants to see their partner's brutal side? What about pee breaks? Who goes first?

Soph's seen the world change beyond recognition, and yet he craves a car and faster home deliveries. What's best? Should we strictly ration the things breaking the planet, do we go medieval on our own asses and suffer while the world repairs, if it can?

As I continue with these books, somehow finding myself writing urban fantasy in a world that now seems entirely possible, I keep wondering if something like this is due sooner than we might think. After all, the world already went into lockdown for over a year, now "they" know it's possible. Maybe it's because the news has recently gone into overdrive about climate change. Every day the UK has one problem or another. Not enough haulage drivers, insufficient workers to pick fruit and veg, dry summers, wet summers, early frosts, spring that is unseasonably cold, mild winters.

The revelations Soph keeps getting might be nothing, or maybe they're something. But how do you find out the truth when you don't want to know the truth? He needs to keep a low profile if he's to survive. After all, it's years until

Jen will be able to fend for herself. But he's known, seemingly without him realizing, and that's a problem in and of itself. It comes with the territory of living a long time —you get about a bit, and Necros have long memories.

I'm having a blast writing this, and the ideas for future books are arriving thick and fast. There are a lot of family members we haven't heard of yet, plus Phage's mum—she's trouble, I can tell. I'm concerned about Jen. How will she react when she hears the truth about what her parents do? And what's in store for her when she's of age? Now that's a conversation you don't want to have with your child. How long can they put off telling her? She's a headstrong girl and smart too, with a lot of emerging gifts, so will find out soon whether they like it or not.

Shey Redgold is sure to be a handful. I can feel it in my bones. Will he ever give up the remote? And will Soph get his chair back?

What the hell is Job up to? It's driving me nuts!

And what's Soph got against the fae? If they're so bad, why did he palm it off on his wife? I think he's up to something there.

Tyr's going to be a right handful, but Soph seems to have a handle on him. For now. Kind of.

As for Woofer? What can I say? I love the little guy. But what's all this about him suddenly being able to morph? How'd he acquire that gift? I already know, but I'm not telling. You'll find out soon enough though! And is it just him, or are all dogs so nutty when it comes to balls? I think we all know the answer to that one. Maybe he'll let go of the ball and can finally play fetch. Although, I wouldn't put money on it.

Come on, let's all have a break together. Ready?

"Play ball with Woofer?"

"Okay, be right with you. Drop. Drop! I said, drop the bloody ball!"

See you next time in Dragon Nights.

Stay jiggy,

Al

p.s. Don't forget, you can get notified of new notes and never miss a new release. Sign up at alkline.co.uk. We've got a lot of ground to cover, and a lot of unanswered questions.

Printed in Great Britain
by Amazon